THE WORLD OF
NORM
MUST END SOON

ORCHARD BOOKS

First published in Great Britain in 2017 by The Watts Publishing Group

1 3 5 7 9 10 8 6 4 2

Text copyright © Jonathan Meres, 2017
Illustrations copyright © Donough O'Malley, 2017

A CIP catalogue record for this book
is available from the British Library.

ISBN 978 1 40834 603 7

Printed and bound in Great Britain
by CPI Group (UK) Ltd, Croydon, CR0 4YY

The paper and board used in this book are
made from wood from responsible sources.

MIX
Paper from
responsible sources
FSC® C104740

Orchard Books
An imprint of
Hachette Children's Group
Part of The Watts Publishing Group Limited
Carmelite House
50 Victoria Embankment
London EC4Y 0DZ
An Hachette UK Company
www.hachette.co.uk
www.hachettechildrens.co.uk

JONATHAN MERES

THE WORLD OF NORM

MUST END SOON

ORCHARD

This one's for Max, Ollie & Noah, again.
My very own Norm, Brian & Dave.

CHAPTER 1

Norm knew it was going to be one of those days
when he woke up and found himself about to pee
in his **mum's** wardrobe. Not that
he actually **knew** it was his
mum's wardrobe, of course.
Or **anybody's** wardrobe, for
that matter. All **Norm** knew
was that he needed to
pee. And pee was precisely
what he intended to do.
And pretty flipping soon,
too.

"STOP!" yelled a voice.

Uh? thought Norm, still
half asleep. If not slightly
more. Who **was** that?

And what were they doing, watching him go to the flipping toilet? Couldn't a guy get **any** privacy around here? Apparently **not**.

"NORMAN!" yelled the same voice.

"Yeah?" croaked Norm, like a frog with flu.

"What do you think you're **doing**, love?" said a different, altogether more **gentle** voice.

Norm thought for a moment. Firstly, just how many people were **in** the bathroom? Because it was **beginning** to feel like the whole flipping **street** were in there. And secondly, what did they **think**

he was doing? Was this some kind of trick question? Or just a really **stupid** one? Either way, he still needed to pee. Because if he **didn't** pee, there was a very good chance that he'd burst. And if **that** happened, things could get **really** messy. Literally.

Norm suddenly saw the light. Or strictly speaking, Norm suddenly saw a **bedside** light, reflected in a mirror, a fraction of a second after it was switched on. Lying next to the light was Norm's mum. And lying next to his mum was his dad.

"Oh, hi," said Norm, turning around and finally realising where he was. And, much more importantly, realising where he **wasn't**.

"Never mind 'hi'," said Norm's dad, grumpily. "Have you any idea what time it is?"

7

Not only did Norm **not** have any idea what flipping time it was, he couldn't care **less** what flipping time it was. All he knew was that if he didn't pee soon he was going to wet himself.

"I'll tell you, shall I? It's four o'clock in the morning! **That's** what time it is!"

Norm sighed. So if his dad knew all along, why flipping ask?

"This isn't the **first** time this has happened, is it, Norman?"

"It's the second time, actually," added Norm's mum, helpfully. "Except the *last* time, it was your dad's wardrobe, not mine."

"'S'not *my* fault," said Norm.

"Oh, really?" said Norm's dad, the vein on the side of his head beginning to throb – a sure-fire sign that he was getting stressed. Not that Norm noticed. Or *ever* noticed. "And why's that, then?"

"Toilet's moved," muttered Norm.

"Pardon?" said Norm's dad.

"Toilet's moved!" said Norm, a little bit louder. "'S'not where it used to be."

"I heard you the *first* time, Norman."

Gordon flipping Bennet, thought Norm. So why get him to repeat it, then? Was it *him*, or was his dad making even **less** sense than usual? And **that** was flipping saying something! Because his dad made about as much sense as a flipping jellyfish, at the **best** of times. And not a very **intelligent** jellyfish, either.

"I'm getting a strange sense of déjà vu, here," said Norm's dad.

That settled it, as far as Norm was concerned. His dad had started talking an entirely different **language**. He'd lost the plot completely. Assuming he'd ever actually **had** the plot in the first place.

"We've had this conversation before," said Norm's dad.

"Almost word for word, actually," said his mum. "I remember it like it was yesterday. But it wasn't."

"It wasn't the *toilet* that moved!" Norm's dad went on. "It was *us* that moved!"

"Several months ago," said Norm's mum.

"Do you not *remember*?" said his dad, sounding more and more exasperated.

Norm sighed again. Did he remember having this *conversation* before? Or did he remember moving *house*? If his dad wanted a straight answer, then he really needed to be more specific.

"Well?" said Norm's dad.

Norm shrugged. "'S'not *my* fault."

"Will you *please* stop saying that?" said Norm's dad.

"Well, it's *not,*" said Norm.

"Well, it's certainly not *my* fault!" said Norm's dad.

"Huh," harrumphed Norm quietly to himself. But clearly not quietly enough.

"What was that?" said Norm's dad.

"It's OK," said Norm's mum, who, luckily, *could* tell when Norm's dad was getting stressed and who, as usual, was doing her best to act as peacemaker.

"No, it's *not* OK, actually," said Norm's dad. "Have you got something to say to me, Norman?"

Norm thought for a moment. Had he got something to say, to his *dad*? Where did he flipping start?

"Well?" said Norm's dad, expectantly. "I'm waiting."

Norm glanced at his mum, who seemed to be staring back at him with an almost pleading expression in her eyes. As if she was desperately trying to communicate something to him, telepathically. As if she didn't want him to actually **say** whatever it was that she thought he might be about to say.

"I really need to pee," said Norm, hopping from one foot to the other.

Norm's dad regarded Norm, for a second or two. "Is that what you were going to say?"

Norm nodded. "Yeah."

Norm's dad sighed. "Off you go then. And don't let this happen again."

Norm closed the wardrobe door and began heading towards the *real* toilet. He'd do his *best* to make sure it didn't happen again. But there was no guarantee that it *wouldn't*.

CHAPTER 2

It was several hours before Norm woke up again. But this time, it was morning.

Whether it was the shaft of sunlight shining through the crack in the curtains and bouncing off his eyelids that woke him, or whether it was just the increased noise levels from elsewhere in the house, Norm wasn't entirely sure. Not that it mattered. All Norm knew was that he was no longer asleep.

Which was flipping annoying for a start. Well, as far as **Norm** was concerned it was flipping annoying, anyway. Because somewhere at the back of his mind, Norm was vaguely aware that he needed *more* sleep, not *less*. That **something** had happened during the night. But what?

Norm continued to lie in bed. Well, at least he **presumed** it was his bed, anyway. But until he could actually be bothered to open his eyes and *check*, he wouldn't know for sure. After all, there'd been that one time in IKEA when he lay down and the next thing he knew, he'd nodded off, only to find a crowd of strangers staring at him when he woke up again, cooing and smiling, as if he was some kind of cute baby animal in a flipping **zoo**. His parents, on the other hand, hadn't found it cute at all. They'd been worried sick and told him in no uncertain

terms not to go wandering off by himself again. Bit harsh, looking back on it now, thought Norm, because he must have only been about three at the time. But then he'd also been an only child at the time, so he could understand his mum and dad being a **bit** anxious. Because those were the days when he was the centre of their universe. Before his stupid little brothers came along and ruined everything for ever. Even so, it wasn't like he'd wandered off into the flipping **jungle** all by himself. The **biggest** danger he faced in IKEA was getting lost in the flipping kitchen department. Either that or being **bored** to death. How his parents actually went there **voluntarily** was beyond Norm's comprehension. But then, his parents were in their forties. And people did weird stuff when they were **that** old.

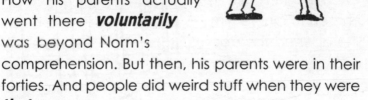

There was a knock on the door. Which did little to improve Norm's mood. If anything, it made it even **worse**. Why did people have to knock on doors, anyway? They were **so** flipping annoying. Why couldn't they just leave him alone? And if they really **had** to disturb him, why couldn't they phone up first and make an appointment? And how about they ring a flipping **bell**, instead of flipping **knocking**?

"Can I come in, love?" said a muffled voice.

"I dunno," grumbled Norm. "Can you?"

Whether Norm's mum misheard Norm, or whether she'd merely chosen to ignore him, she opened the door and came in anyway.

"Morning, sleepyhead."

"Are you sure?" said Norm, **finally** opening his eyes.

"Am I sure, **what**?" said Norm's mum, perching on the end of the bed.

"That it's morning?"

Norm's mum laughed. "Yes, I'm sure."

"Positive?"

Norm's mum nodded. "Positive."

"Prove it."

"Pardon?"

"Prove it," said Norm again.

"Prove what?" said Norm's mum.

"That it's morning."

"You actually want me to **prove** that it's morning?"

"Yeah," said Norm.

"How?"

Norm thought for a moment. "Dunno."

"Well, neither do I," said his mum. "You'll just have to take my word for it."

Norm yawned like a hippo, waking from hibernation. Not that Norm had ever actually **seen** a hippo yawn before. And he had no idea whether hippos hibernated, either. But that wasn't the point. The point was that he was still abso-flipping-lutely **pooped**.

Norm's mum smiled. "I take it you dropped off again, then?"

Dropped off? thought Norm. Dropped off what? And where? What was his mum on about?

"You got back to sleep?"

"Oh, right," said Norm, twigging. "*Erm*, yeah. S'pose so."

Norm's mum looked at Norm. "You don't remember, do you?"

Uh? thought Norm. He didn't remember *what*? The precise moment he went to sleep? Well of *course* he didn't! What was he supposed to do? Take a flipping *selfie*, to remind himself?

"Your ... nocturnal ramble?"

"My *what*?" said Norm, pulling a face like a cat's bottom.

"Your little night-time stroll?"

Gordon flipping *Bennet*, thought Norm. Why couldn't she just *say* whatever she was *trying* to say, instead of talking like she'd swallowed a flipping *dictionary*?

"When you, erm ..."

"When I *what*?" said Norm.

"Relieved yourself in my wardrobe?"

"Uh?" said Norm.

"Peed," said his mum. "Or *nearly* peed, anyway."

"Seriously?" said Norm.

"Seriously, love. But you managed to stop yourself, just in time."

So *that* was what had happened during the night, thought Norm. He *knew* there was *something*. He just couldn't quite put his finger on it.

"Soooo ..."

"What?" said Norm.

"I don't suppose you remember the conversation you had with your father, either, then?"

"When?" said Norm.

"At four o'clock this morning. When you nearly peed in my wardrobe."

Uh? thought Norm. If he couldn't remember nearly peeing in his mum's wardrobe, he was hardly likely to remember a flipping conversation he'd had with his dad at the same flipping *time*, was he?

"What was it about, Mum?"

"Doesn't matter," said Norm's mum quickly.

Uh? thought Norm, again. So if it didn't *matter*, what was the flipping point of *mentioning* it, then?

"It's just that ..."

Just that *what*? thought Norm. For some reason his mum seemed reluctant to continue. But eventually she did.

"You shouldn't be *too* quick to blame him, you know."

"Sorry, what, Mum?" said Norm, by now more than just a tad confused.

"For moving," said Norm's mum.

"*Moving*?" said Norm.

"House," said his mum. "Don't be *too* quick to blame your dad."

Too quick? thought Norm. What did she mean, too *quick*? *First* of all, they'd moved house *ages* ago. And *second* of all, it *was* his flipping dad's fault. After all, it was his *dad* who'd lost his job, not *him*. It was his *dad* who'd blown loads of money, not *him*. As far as *Norm* was concerned, his dad was a *hundred* per cent responsible for them having to move. If not *more*.

"Don't you think he feels bad enough already, love?"

Norm shrugged. Or at least *tried* to. But it wasn't easy, shrugging whilst lying in bed. And anyway, what kind of ridiculous question was *that*? How was *he* supposed to know how his *dad* felt? Norm knew how *he* felt. He felt angry. Angry because they'd had to leave their *old* house. Angry because he never had any money to pimp up his mountain bike. Angry because he was expected to eat supermarket own-brand Coco Pops for the rest of his flipping life, instead of *proper* Coco Pops like they did before. Angry because ... because ... well, because things just weren't like they used to be. Not that things were ever particularly *amazing*

before. They were never, ever rich beyond Norm's wildest dreams. That would be virtually **impossible**. But it wasn't like they used to live in a palace, or anything. It was just a normal-sized house. A normal-sized house with normal-sized rooms and a normal-sized garden. And a normal-sized drive to ride his bike up and down. Not like **now**. Everything was so much **smaller** now. Like their old house had shrunk in the wash. And it just wasn't **flipping** fair.

"I'll tell you then, shall I?" said Norm's mum, when it became obvious that Norm wasn't going to reply. "He **does** feel bad. Really bad. And the last thing he needs right now is for anyone to **remind** him."

Great, thought Norm. He hadn't even got out of bed yet and already he was being given a flipping

lecture. Didn't exaclly bode well for the **rest** of the day, did it?

"OK?" said his mum.

"Whatever," said Norm, attempting another horizontal shrug.

"Things can only get better, you know."

"Can I have that in writing, please?" said Norm.

Norm's mum smiled. "Look, I understand your frustration."

Norm seriously doubted that. **No** one could understand his frustration. Especially not someone as **ancient** as his mum.

"No, really I do," said his mum. "I was your age once."

Norm seriously doubted **that**, too. Or at least he found it difficult to **imagine** that his mum had ever been his age.

"Can you believe that you're actually going to be thirteen soon, love?"

Norm thought for a moment. Actually, no. Now his mum came to mention it, he **couldn't** believe it.

"You seem to have been **nearly** thirteen for ever!" laughed his mum.

"Tell me about it," grunted Norm.

"That must be why you need so much **sleep**. Because you're almost a teenager!"

No, thought Norm. The reason he needed so much sleep was because he'd been up till after midnight, looking at mountain biking videos on YouTube. And waking up about to pee in his mum's wardrobe probably hadn't helped much, either.

"Hang on," said Norm's mum. "What's that, above your lip?"

"My nose?" said Norm.

"No. **Below** your nose," said Norm's mum. "Looks like a bit of ..."

"A bit of **what**?"

"Facial hair."

Uh? thought Norm. So he was growing a flipping **moustache**? First he knew about it. Why hadn't anyone said anything before? How come he was always the last to find out about these things?

Not that he'd ever actually **grown** a moustache before. Or anything else for that matter. But that wasn't the point. The point was, it was flipping **typical**.

"Oh no, wait," said Norm's mum, examining Norm more closely.

"What?" said Norm.

"That's **disgusting**."

What was disgusting? wondered Norm, his imagination beginning to run riot. Well, maybe not actually **run** riot. But **walk** riot, anyway. **Running** riot was way too much like hard work, first thing in the morning. Or any time for that matter.

"It's pasta sauce," said his mum.

"Pasta sauce?"

Norm stuck his tongue out and licked, just above his mouth.

"Oh yeah. That's not disgusting, Mum. It's quite nice actually."

"I meant it's disgusting that it's still *there*!" said Norm's mum. "It means you didn't wash properly last night."

Norm thought for a moment. He hadn't washed at *all* last night, let alone properly. But he figured now probably wasn't the best time to mention that.

Norm's mum smiled and shook her head. "I don't know, love. What am I going to do with you?"

What was she going to *do* with him? thought Norm.

How about leave him alone and let him go back to sleep? That would be a flipping start.

"Are you going to get up and have breakfast at some point?"

"Dunno," said Norm. "Do I have a choice?"

"Not really, no," said his mum.

Gordon flipping **Bennet**, thought Norm. So why flipping **ask**, then?

"Oh, come on, love," said Norm's mum. "It's not **that** bad, is it?"

Maybe not **yet**, it wasn't, thought Norm. Bul the day was still young.

CHAPTER 3

By the time Norm had licked the rest of the pasta sauce off his face and got dressed, it very nearly **wasn't** time for breakfast at all. In fact, by the time Norm had licked the rest of the pasta sauce off his face and got dressed, it was nearer **lunchtime** than **breakfast** time. But that was OK. At least it **was** pasta sauce and not the first signs of a moustache. Which was a relief, as far as **Norm** was concerned.

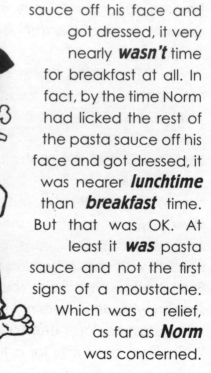

Because the last thing he wanted was to turn into a flipping **werewolf**.

"Table for one?" said Norm's dad, looking up from his paper, as Norm stumbled into the kitchen like a sleep-deprived zombie.

"What?" mumbled Norm groggily. "Er, yeah, all right then."

"Well, tough luck," said Norm's dad. "What do you think this is? A **restaurant**, or something?"

Norm briefly **thought** about saying something, but didn't. Not because he didn't think he **ought** to say something. He'd have **loved** to say something suitably witty, or something withering, to his dad. Even better, he'd have loved to say something suitably witty **and** withering, to his dad. The problem was he just couldn't **think** of anything, that was all. Which was annoying for a flipping start. But what

was even **more** annoying was the fact that Norm knew he'd probably think of something later on. But by then it would be too late. It would be a bit like ... like ... like ... Norm sighed with frustration. He couldn't even think what it would be a bit like. He'd probably think of **that** later on, too. Which made it **doubly** flipping annoying.

"You'll just have to sit here with the rest of us, I'm afraid," said Norm's dad.

"Yeah, Norman!" trilled Norm's middle brother, Brian.

"Yeah, Norman!" echoed Norm's little brother, Dave, but a little bit higher.

"Shut up, you little freaks!" hissed Norm.

"Language!" said Dave.

"Would sir like to see the sauce list?" said Brian, in a funny, posh voice.

Norm pulled a face. "What?"

"We have red sauce, brown sauce or white sauce."

"White sauce?" said Dave.

"Mayonnaise," explained Brian.

"Oh, right, yeah!" giggled Dave. "Good one."

Gordon flipping **Bennet**, thought Norm. Was it too early to go back to bed yet? Or emigrate. Norm wasn't overly fussed which. As long as it meant spending less time with Brian and Dave, or preferably **no** time at all. Because his backside hadn't even made contact with a seat yet, but **already** they were doing his flipping **head** in.

"Can I have my breakfast somewhere else?" said Norm.

"Like where?" said his dad.

Norm shrugged. "Belgium?"

"Belgium?" said Dave.

"Brussels," said Brian.

"Brussels?" said Dave, screwing up his face in

disgust. "Aw, yuk! I thought they had **waffles** for breakfast, in Belgium!"

"What?" said Brian. "No! I meant Brussels is the **capital** of Belgium!"

"Oh, **right**!" laughed Dave.

"You **wombat**!" said Brian.

"No, **you're** a wombat, Brian!" said Dave.

"No, **you're** a wombat, Dave!" said Brian.

Norm exhaled slowly and noisily.

"You sound like you've got a **leak**, Norman!" said Brian.

"Oh yeah?" said Norm. "Well, you sound like ... like ..."

"What?" said Brian.

"Like ... like ..."

"I'm waiting," said Brian.

Norm was waiting, too. Waiting for the day when he no longer had to put up with his stupid, smelly little brothers, spouting a never-ending stream of nonsense, as if there was some kind of competition to see who could talk the most rubbish. Honestly, it was hard to believe they were members of the same *species* sometimes, let alone the same flipping *family*.

"Well?" said Brian.

"Well, *what*?" said Norm.

"I'm still waiting."

"Ooh, *while* we're waiting," said Dave, "what was that noise last night?"

"What noise?" said Brian. "You mean Dad snoring?"

"No," said Dave.

"Well, what was it, then?" said Brian.

"I don't *know*," said Dave. "That's why I'm *asking*!"

Brian nodded. "Fair enough. Good point, Dave."

"You wombat," said Dave.

"No, *you're* a wombat," said Brian.

"No, *you're* a wombat, Brian," said Dave.

"You mean the noise at four o'clock this morning?"

said Norm's dad.

"I don't think we need to go into that, right now, do we?" said Norm's mum, appearing in the doorway at that moment and ushering Norm towards the table. "Sit down and have your breakfast, love. There's a good boy."

Norm did as he was told and sat down at the table. And despite the fact that this meant sitting opposite his brothers, he was secretly quite glad. Because at least he'd been spared the ultimate humiliation of Brian and Dave finding out about him mistaking his mum's wardrobe for a toilet. Because he needed *that* about as much as he needed a spare elbow. And actually, thought Norm, the sooner he got breakfast over with, the sooner he could escape this insanity. If only for a while.

Norm picked up the box of Coco Pops and gave it a shake. It sounded suspiciously empty. Peering inside, confirmed his worst fears.

"Got any more?"

"Any more what, love?" said Norm's mum.

"Any more Coco Pops," said Norm.

"Any more Coco Pops, **what**?" said Norm's dad.

Norm pulled a face. As far as **he** was concerned, that was the end of the sentence. He'd said all he wanted to say.

"Any more Coco Pops, **please**?" said his dad.

"Uh?" said Norm. "Oh, right, yeah. Any more Coco Pops, **please**, Mum?"

"No. Sorry, love."

"WHAAAAAAAAT?" bellowed Norm, like a moose giving birth.

"We're fresh out," said Norm's mum.

"BUT ..."

"You heard your mother," snapped Norm's dad.

Norm's dad was right. Norm **had** heard his mother. They were fresh out of Coco Pops. And not even **proper** Coco Pops, either. Supermarket own-brand flipping Coco Pops. Were things really **that** bad? It would appear that they were.

"Sorry, Norman," said Dave.

"Uh?" said Norm. "What do you mean, you're sorry? What for?"

"For finishing them."

"It's your own fault," said Norm's dad.

No one said anything, for a few seconds. Norm turned to see his dad glaring at him, like an owl sizing up a mouse.

"Sorry, Dad, were you talking to me?"

"Who do you *think* I was talking to?" said Norm's dad.

"But …"

"What?"

"You think it's *my* fault?"

"You do the maths, Norman."

Gordon flipping *Bennet*, thought Norm. He was used to being blamed for just about **everything**, but *this* was ridiculous! And what exactly had flipping *maths* got to do with Coco Pops? He was *rubbish* at maths.

"How come?" said Brian.

"How come what?" said Norm's dad.

"How come it's **Norman's** fault that Dave and I finished the Coco Pops? He wasn't even *here*."

Norm looked at Brian with a kind of grudging respect. He could be superhumanly annoying at times – in fact never mind '*at times*', Brian could be superhumanly annoying pretty much **all** the time – but every once in a while, he said something that **didn't** make Norm immediately want to scream at the top of his voice and run down the street tearing his own hair out. And it looked like he just **might** have done that now. How **could** it be Norm's fault if he hadn't been here in the first flipping place?

"What I **meant**," said Norm's dad, "was that if Norman had got out of bed a bit **earlier**, there might have been some Coco Pops **left** and we wouldn't have been having this conversation!"

"But ..." began Norm.

"No buts!" said his dad, cutting him off.

Dave giggled.

Brian shook his head. "Not *that* kind of but."

"What?" said Dave.

"But with *one* 't' not *two*!"

"Oh," said Dave.

"Honestly, Dave, that's so *immature*," said Brian.

Dave shrugged. "I'm only seven. What do you expect?"

Brian thought for a moment. "Fair enough. That's another good point, Dave."

"You wombat," said Dave.

"No, *you're* a wombat, Dave," said Brian.

"No, *you're* a wombat!" said Dave.

"That's quite enough, you two!" said Norm's mum, sharply.

"What are we going to do, Mum?" said Norm.

"About what?" said Norm's mum.

"The Coco Pops?"

Norm's mum smiled. "We'll get some on the way back."

Norm pulled a face. "Who will?"

"We will."

"We?" said Norm.

"Your dad and I."

"On the way back from where?"

"Oh, sorry, love. Didn't we tell you?"

Norm sighed. How was he supposed to know what his mum and dad hadn't told him, if his mum hadn't told him whatever it was that she hadn't told him? Why did everything always have to be so flipping complicated?

"Your mother and I have got to go out for a while," said Norm's dad.

"Where to?" said Norm, instantly anxious, like a meerkat suddenly sensing danger.

"Can't say," said his dad.

"Can't you pronounce it?" said Dave.

Norm's dad looked at Dave. "Pardon?"

"Is that why you can't say where you're going?" said Dave. "Because you can't pronounce it?"

Norm's dad laughed. "No!"

"How do you spell it?" said Brian. "Perhaps *I* can pronounce it."

"No, I meant, that's *not* why I can't say," said Norm's dad. "I just can't say, that's all."

But by now, Norm had stopped listening. Because there was only *one* thing on his mind. One thing, which *could* have a hu-flipping-*mongous* impact on the rest of his day.

"You *are* taking Brian and Dave, right, Mum?"

"What, love?"

"You're taking Brian and Dave with you, right? To wherever it is that you're going? Even though you can't say where it is?"

"Erm, no, actually we're not, love," said Norm's mum. "We're leaving them with you."

"WHAAAAAAAAAAAAAAT?" bellowed Norm, like an entire *herd* of moose giving birth.

Norm's mum looked at Norm. "Is that a problem?"

Was that a problem? thought Norm. Was that a flipping problem? Was his mum completely and utterly off her **rocker**? Had she temporarily forgotten that it was **Saturday**? More importantly, had she temporarily forgotten what Norm always **did** on Saturdays? He went **biking** on Saturdays! With **Mikey**! And had done ever since dinosaurs roamed the earth! Well, maybe not quite **that** long. But for as long as they could balance on two wheels, without the need for stabilisers, anyway. Norm and Mikey, that is. Not dinosaurs. But that wasn't the point. The point was that this was **indeed** a problem. And no **ordinary**-sized problem, either. This was a **planet**-sized problem. A planet-sized problem with flipping **knobs** on! In short, thought Norm, this was an abso-flipping-lute **disaster!**

Norm's mum smiled. "It won't be for long, love. Just a couple of hours."

A couple of **hours**? thought Norm. That might not seem long, to someone as prehistoric as his **mum**, but at that precise moment it seemed like an entire flipping **lifetime** to him. **Anything** could happen in a couple of hours. Literally **anything**. Like ...like ...well, like literally **anything**. The day was rapidly going from bad to catas-flipping-**trophic** and he'd only just got up! His parents might as well have announced

that they were going away and never coming back! In fact, why didn't they just lock him in his room and throw away the flipping key? Because this was the end of his world, as Norm knew it. Like some kind of horror movie, come chillingly to life.

"Thanks, love," said Norm's mum. "I knew you'd understand."

Norm gawped at his mum like a gobsmacked goldfish. What was she talking about? Understand?

He didn't understand at all! He might as well have been having a conversation with a flipping **microwave**. It just wasn't fair. Why did **he** have to stay at home, looking after his stupid, stinky brothers, when he **could** be whizzing in and out of trees, on his bike, in the woods behind the shopping precinct? In fact, never mind **could** be, thought Norm. Flipping well **should** be. In fact, never mind **should** be, thought Norm. Flipping well **would** be, if he had anything to do with it.

"I can't," said Norm.

The temperature in the room suddenly seemed to plummet. The atmosphere was already somewhat frosty. But now it was positively arctic. The silence was almost deafening. And had Norm actually **wanted** to, he could have cut the tension with a knife.

"Pardon?" said his dad, the vein on the side of his head, beginning to throb. Not that Norm noticed.

"I can't stay here," said Norm.

"Can't?" said Norm's dad. "Or won't?"

Both, actually, thought Norm.

"We thought you'd appreciate the extra responsibility, love," said Norm's mum. "After all, you're …"

"Nearly thirteen," said Norm, cutting her off. "Yeah, I know, Mum. But …"

"Uh-uh," said his dad, wagging a warning finger. "I said no *buts*."

This time, however, there was no giggling from Dave. Or anyone else for that matter. Least of all from Norm, who felt that he was about to spontaneously combust and burst into flames. Not that Norm had ever actually spontaneously combusted before. But he imagined this must be what it felt like. And it wasn't a very pleasant

feeling. But that wasn't the point. The point was he *didn't* want any extra responsibility. In fact, he didn't particularly want any responsibility at all, let alone *extra* responsibility.

"*Why* can't you?" said Norm's mum.

"Because I'm going *biking*!" said Norm. "With *Mikey*!"

"Correction," said Norm's dad. "You **were** going biking with Mikey. And don't answer back!"

Norm sighed.

"And you can cut *that* out, too, Norman!"

"Cut *what* out?" said Norm.

"All that huffing and puffing!" said his dad. "You're staying and looking after your brothers. And that's all there is to it!"

"Yeah, Norman!" shrieked Brian, like a parrot with beak-ache.

"Yeah, Norman!" echoed Dave, but a little bit higher.

Gordon flipping **Bennet**, thought Norm. If this was a sign of things to come, then someone had better call the flipping fire brigade. And quick. Because at this rate, he really **was** going to spontaneously combust, any second now.

CHAPTER 4

Most people would have assumed that their day couldn't possibly go any more pear-shaped and rubbish. And rightly so. Because for *most* people, it probably *couldn't*. But Norm wasn't *most* people. Norm knew, only too well, that just because he'd woken up at stupid o'clock, about to pee in his mum's wardrobe, and just because he'd been told that he couldn't do the *one* thing in the whole wide world that he loved doing more than *anything* else, not to mention the lack of proper Coco Pops – or *any* kind of Coco Pops for that matter – *didn't* necessarily mean that things couldn't get even worse than they already were. Because from nearly thirteen years of bitter personal experience, Norm knew only too well that they flipping could. And sure enough, before too long, they flipping *did*.

Not that Norm walking into his room and discovering John, the stinky cockapoo, fast asleep and dribbling on his pillow, was *that* much of a disaster, in the great scheme of things. Because it wasn't. It was just some stupid dog, after all. But on top of everything else? It was the *last* thing Norm needed right then. Or *any* time for that matter.

"GERROFF!" roared Norm, like a livid lion.

Not only did John not **gerroff**, he didn't bat an eyelid, let alone move a muscle. Whether this was simply because he was so sound asleep that he just didn't **hear** Norm, or whether it was because John's previous owners were Polish and he still hadn't fully mastered the English language yet, Norm wasn't sure. Not that Norm cared. And not that he actually **owned** John, either. Strictly speaking, John belonged to Brian and Dave. He'd been given to them as some kind of so-called 'reward' for moving house and to somehow make them

feel **better** and help them to cope with all the 'upheaval'. Which even now Norm still couldn't quite get his head around. Because the only thing **he'd** got when they'd moved house, was flipping **angry**. And **flipping angry** had been his default setting pretty much ever since. But that's what happened when you were no longer king of the castle and you no longer ruled the roost. Not that

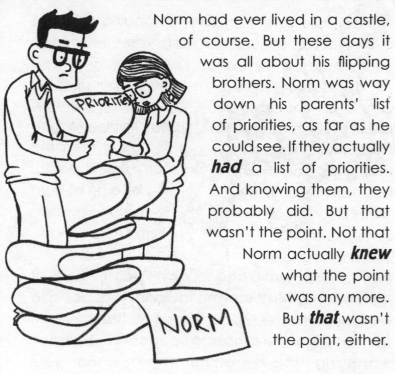

Norm had ever lived in a castle, of course. But these days it was all about his flipping brothers. Norm was way down his parents' list of priorities, as far as he could see. If they actually **had** a list of priorities. And knowing them, they probably did. But that wasn't the point. Not that Norm actually **knew** what the point was any more. But **that** wasn't the point, either.

"Stupid flipping dog," muttered Norm to himself.

John immediately opened his eyes and looked straight at Norm.

"Oh, you understood **that**, then?" said Norm.

"WOOF!" went John, wagging his tail, like an out-of-control windscreen wiper.

"Gordon flipping **Bennet**," sighed Norm.

John responded by panting furiously, his drooling tongue lolling from the corner of his mouth, like a bit of ham trying to escape from a sandwich.

Norm sighed again and shook his head wearily. If he hadn't **already** known that today was going to be one of those days, he flipping did **now**. In fact, the way things were shaping up, it looked like today was going to be like all the other days that were going to be one of those days, rolled into one. So how come he **didn't** feel as if his head was going to explode, like he normally would? How come, for once, he felt that there was no point getting all stressed about it? And most worryingly, how come he was suddenly aware of a strange sensation in his cheeks? Some kind of twitch in muscles that he'd long since forgotten he even **had**, let alone known what they were actually **for**?

Whack, whack, whack! went John's tail, on Norm's pillow.

By now, Norm no longer felt in full control of his own face. Whatever it was that was happening felt most peculiar. He hadn't experienced anything like it for as long as he could remember. Not that he could remember all that long. But that wasn't the point. The point was that usually he would have erupted like a flipping **volcano** by now. But tor some reason, he still hadn't.

Thump, thump, thump! went John's tail. Thwack, thwack, thwack!

It was at that moment that Norm happened to glance up at a framed poster hanging on the wall. It was a poster of one of his all-time favourite

mountain bikers, hurtling down a terrifyingly steep hillside, frozen in mid-air like some kind of pedal-powered superhero. Norm had spent literally **days** of his life gazing at the photo and imagining that it was him posing for the cameras instead. But not now. Because Norm had just noticed something. His face, reflected in the glass. And all of a sudden, he knew exactly what that strange, alien sensation in his cheeks was.

He was smiling. OK, so it was just the faintest **glimmer** of a smile. Scarcely visible from the other side of the **room**, let alone from **space**. But nevertheless, he could definitely detect a very slight upward curve on each side of his mouth. Unbelievably, considering the day he'd had so far, he'd actually found something vaguely amusing. And even more unbelievably, the thing that Norm had found vaguely **amusing** turned out to be the **dog**! This was **almost** unheard of. In fact, never mind **almost** unheard of. It was **completely** unheard of. To the best of Norm's knowledge, he'd **never** found John even **remotely** amusing, before. Quite the opposite in fact. Norm had always found John intensely **unamusing**. Not to mention revolting. OK, so maybe not **quite** so unamusing and revolting as his **brothers**. Then again, there was practically **nothing** Norm found more unamusing or revolting than his brothers. But even so. He couldn't deny that, just for the very briefest of moments, he **had** actually cracked just the teensiest of smiles.

So, what on earth was going on? wondered Norm. Was he ill? Was it something he'd eaten? Or rather, was it something that he **hadn't** eaten? Like **proper** flipping food, for instance? Had several months of hardship and supermarket own-brand Coco Pops **finally** taken thier toll and turned his brain to mashed

potato? It was the only possible explanation **Norm** could think of. Well, apart from being abducted by aliens the previous night and having his brain swapped for an entirely **different** brain. But surely even **he** would have remembered **that**, thought Norm. Then again, maybe he wouldn't. Because maybe the whole point of being abducted by aliens and having your brain swapped was that you **couldn't** remember anything about it? Either way, it was a weird feeling – and actually quite unsettling – for Norm to suddenly find himself **smiling**. No matter **how** small the smile was.

Norm turned around again. John was still staring

gormlessly up at him. And **still** panting like an athlete gasping for breath after smashing the world record for the hundred metres.

"What?" said Norm irritably.

"WOOF!" went John, wagging his tail faster than ever.

"Gordon flipping **Bennet**!" said Norm. "Just because I flipping **smiled**, doesn't mean I **like** you. Doesn't mean we're suddenly best friends, or anything. So don't go getting any ideas, right? Because ..."

Norm stopped, mid-sentence, as the reality of the situation gradually dawned on him. Well, not so much gradually **dawned** on him, as suddenly hit him, full in the face, as if he'd walked slap-bang into a brick wall. And the reality of the situation **was** that right now, he should have been out on his bike enjoying himself and, more importantly, perfecting his skills so that he could one day achieve his ultimate dream and long-held ambition of becoming World Mountain Biking Champion. And what was he *actually* doing? He was stuck in his bedroom, talking to a flipping *dog*. Or talking *at* a dog, anyway. He doubted very much whether the dog had understood a single word he'd been saying.

Norm sighed. It really was quite *extraordinarily* unfair the way his parents had just announced what they were going to do – and then just flipping *done* it. They might have at least given him a *bit* of notice. But no. No sooner had the words left their mouths, than *they* left the house! Norm had had virtually no chance to think about it properly. And now that he *had* had a chance to think about it properly, it seemed even *more* flipping unfair. And where had his mum and dad gone, anyway? Why couldn't they just *say*? Why all the flipping *mystery*, like they were going on some top-secret spy mission, or something? As for all that stuff about him 'appreciating the extra responsibility'? What a pile of steaming garbage *that* was. Responsibility was the last flipping thing he wanted. Never mind *extra* responsibility. The only time Norm ever wanted extra anything was if there was an option to have extra *cheese* on his Margherita pizza. Then again, thought Norm, as long as they remembered to get Coco Pops on the way back, maybe he didn't really care. And as long as Brian and Dave didn't keep pestering him and stayed glued to the Xbox, playing Lord of the Nerds or Call of Nature or whatever, maybe looking after them wasn't such a big deal after all?

Norm suddenly stopped thinking. Or rather, he suddenly stopped that particular train of thought and immediately embarked on another one. As long as Brian and Dave were glued to the Xbox, what was stopping *him* nipping out on his bike for a bit? Abso-flipping-lutely *nothing*, as far as Norm could see. It didn't even have to be for long. Just a quick whiz around the block, or something. His brothers need never even *know*. And if *they* didn't know, his mum and dad would never know either, would they? And that was the main thing. Actually, thought Norm, it was the *only* thing.

There was no point thinking about it any longer. Norm had already decided, the nanosecond the idea had popped into his head. It was as if someone had flicked a switch. He was going to do it. And if he was going to do it, he was going to do it *soon*. Because he knew that if he *didn't* do it soon – and that if he started to think about it *too* much – doubts would begin to seep into his head, like swirling fog and he'd start to dwell on the possible consequences if

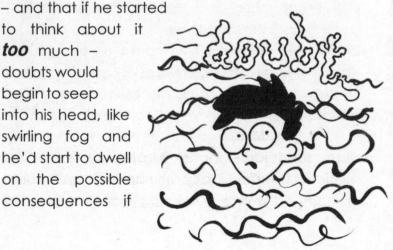

his mum and dad ever **did** find out. And if they ever did find out, there most definitely **would** be consequences. Because there always flipping **were** consequences. Well, at least for **Norm** there were, anyway. His flipping brothers could do just about **anything** and get away with it. They could burn the flipping house down and his parents would just laugh it off as if it was some kind of childish prank that had gone a bit wrong. But if **Norm** did that? He'd never hear the flipping **end** of it! He only had to accidentally burn a slice of flipping **toast** and they'd be banging on about grounding him for life, like he was some kind of hardened criminal.

Norm sniffed a couple of times. Talking about swirling **fog** seeping in, what on **earth** was that smell, he wondered? Well, whatever it was, it was pretty flipping **disgusting**. Like an evil combination of rotten eggs and something that had crawled behind the radiator and died. And whatever it was, he was pretty sure that **he** wasn't responsible for it. If he was, then he'd really got a problem.

Hang on, thought Norm. So if he wasn't responsible for it – and assuming that something hadn't actually crawled behind the radiator and died – that meant ...

"WOOF!" went John, like butter wouldn't melt in his dribbling mouth.

"Gordon flipping **Bennet**!" said Norm, wafting one hand in front of his face and opening the window with his other. "That is un-be-flipping-**lievable**!"

But it wasn't **all** bad news, having a half-Polish cockapoo fart on his pillow, thought Norm. Because if there'd been even the **slightest** doubt whether to sneak out on his bike for a while **before**? There flipping wasn't **now**.

CHAPTER 5

It wasn't *easy*, charging down the stairs, like a herd of elephants, without making as much *noise* as a herd of elephants. Not that Norm had ever actually *heard* a herd of elephants charging down the stairs before. But that wasn't the point. The point *was*, he knew that he needed to get outside as quickly as possible. Not only because he was about to be overcome by the toxic and quite possibly *deadly* fumes emanating from John's bottom, but also because he needed to escape before his brothers figured out what was going on. Because once they *did*, the game would be up, just like that. He wouldn't be able to go biking. Not without Brian and Dave blabbing, anyway. And if they blabbed, who knew what his parents might say, or do? One thing was certain, though, it would be a long time before he was allowed out biking again.

Closing the front door behind him – as *quietly* as possible – Norm breathed in a huge lungful of deliciously fresh and dog-fart-free air. What next? he wondered. Well it was perfectly simple. All he had to do was open the garage door – again, as *quietly* as possible – jump on his bike and ride off into the sunset, like at the end of a movie, where everybody lives happily ever after. Not that the sun was anywhere near *setting* yet, thank goodness. And not that there was much chance of everybody living happily ever after, either. Well, there wasn't much chance of *Norm* living happily ever after, anyway. At least, not *permanently*. The best *he* could hope for was an occasional happy moment here and there, interspersed with the usual setbacks, raised hopes and crushing disappointments. But for now, at least, everything looked rosy. Or *relatively* rosy, anyway.

There was another reason why Norm knew that he needed to get a shift on. The longer he hung around, the more chance there was of him having second thoughts. Because deep down he knew that what he was about to do was wrong. So if his conscience was going to get the better of him, he wanted to be as far away as possible when it happened. That way at least he'd get a decent ride back home. Which wouldn't be great, thought Norm. But it would be better than nothing. Just.

But Norm didn't even get as *far* as the garage door. Because what he *hadn't* bargained for was that the split second he set foot on the drive, a certain *someone* would pop up on the other side of the fence, just like she always flipping did and always flipping had. And sure enough, she flipping *did*.

"Hello, **Norman**!" said Chelsea, in that intensely annoying, sing-song way of hers. Well, intensely annoying for Norm, anyway. Why she had to deliberately overemphasise his name like that, he'd never know. It hadn't been funny the first flipping time. And it hadn't been funny the fifty million times she'd done it *since*, either.

"I said ... hello, **Norman**!" shouted Chelsea, considerably louder.

"Gordon flipping **Bennet**!" muttered Norm. "I heard you the first time!"

"So why didn't you ..."

"SHHHHHHH!" hissed Norm, putting an index finger

to his mouth.

Chelsea looked puzzled. "What?"

"Keep your flipping voice down!" hissed Norm, eyes almost popping out of his head.

"Er, why should I?" said Chelsea.

Norm pulled a face. "What do you mean, why should you? Because I flipping said so. *That's why*!"

Chelsea shrugged. "That's not a *proper* reason."

"What?" said Norm.

"That's not a proper reason," said Chelsea. "And until you actually *give* me a proper reason, I'll talk as loudly as I want to. And anyway *you* can't tell *me* how loud I can talk, *Norman*. It's a free country. And *another* anyway, I don't know if you've noticed, but I'm actually on my **own** drive, not **yours**?"

"Yeah? So?" said Norm.

"So what are you going to do about it?" said Chelsea. "Hmmm?"

"Gordon flipping **Bennet**," muttered Norm again. But only because he couldn't think what else to mutter.

"Well?" said Chelsea expectantly.

"What?" said Norm.

"Have you got a proper reason, or not?"

Norm pulled a face. "For what?"

"Why I should keep my voice down?"

"Oh right," said Norm. "Erm ..."

"Didn't think so," smirked Chelsea.

Norm looked at Chelsea for a moment. "Have you finished?"

"Pardon?"

"Are we done now?"

"You mean, **permanently**?" said Chelsea.

"I **wish**," mumbled Norm.

"What was that, Norman?"

"Nothing," said Norm.

Chelsea smiled. "Exactly."

"Uh?"

"Chelsea one – **Norman** nil."

"What?" said Norm.

"Nothing," said Chelsea.

Norm sighed.

"So, what are you doing, then?" said Chelsea.

Norm shrugged. "Going biking."

"Biking?" said Chelsea, as if Norm had just announced he was pregnant. "What do you want to do *that* for?"

Norm looked at Chelsea as if this was the stupidest question he'd ever heard in his life. And Norm had heard some pretty stupid questions in his time.

"Are you *serious*?"

"Course I'm serious," replied Chelsea.

"What do I want to go *biking* for?"

"Yeah," said Chelsea.

"I don't believe you," said Norm. "You're winding me up."

"I'm not. Honest."

"Yeah, you are."

"OK, maybe I am," said Chelsea. "Let me ask you another question then, **Norman**."

Norm glanced anxiously back towards the house. He knew he was *really* beginning to push his luck now. It could only be a matter of time before his brothers noticed he was gone and came out to investigate.

"Go on then," he said. "Quick."

"What are you doing *later*?"

"Pardon?" said Norm.

"You heard."

Chelsea was right. Norm **had** heard. It was just that this wasn't exactly what he'd been **expecting** to hear. Or even **roughly** what he'd been expecting to hear. Far from it in fact. It had been just about the **last** flipping thing he'd been expecting to hear.

"What am I doing **later**?"

"See?" grinned Chelsea. "I told you you'd heard. And there's no need to look so worried, by the way."

"Why?" said Norm.

"I'm not going to **eat** you, Norman!"

"What?" said Norm. "No. I meant why do you want to know what I'm doing later?"

"No reason in particular," said Chelsea. "Just trying to make polite conversation, that's all."

But there was no **need** for Chelsea to make polite conversation, as far as **Norm** was concerned. In fact, as far as **Norm** was concerned, there was no need for Chelsea to make **any** kind of conversation at all, let alone **polite** conversation. He knew that if he didn't get away in the next couple of minutes, he could probably kiss goodbye to biking, for the foreseeable flipping future. Because never mind his **brothers** coming out to investigate, at this flipping rate his **parents** would be back before he'd even set off!

"Anyway, you're not supposed to answer a question by asking another question."

"Aren't you?" said Norm. "Why not?"

"Ha, ha, very funny," said Chelsea, not smiling.

"Uh?" said Norm.

"Oh, I see," said Chelsea. "So you didn't mean to do that, then?"

Norm looked as blank as the blankest sheet of paper.

"I'll take that as a *no*, then," laughed Chelsea.

"Whatever," said Norm.

They looked at each other for a few moments.

"Well?" said Chelsea eventually breaking the silence.

"Well what?" said Norm.

"What *are* you doing later?"

Norm shrugged. "Nothing much."

Chelsea smiled mysteriously. "That's good."

"What?" said Norm.

"Doesn't matter," said Chelsea. "Don't let me keep you."

Norm eyed his annoying next door neighbour suspiciously. What was she on about? And what exactly did she mean by *keep* him? He had no intention of ever being *kept* by *anyone*, if he could possibly help it. Least of all by flipping Chelsea!

"Off you go!"

"Where to?" said Norm.

"Biking, *silly*!"

"Oh right, yeah," said Norm, as if he'd temporarily **forgotten** what he was supposed to be doing. But if he had, he soon remembered again.

"See you later, **Norman**!" yelled Chelsea, disappearing from view. "Missing you already!"

"SHHHHHH!" hissed Norm, opening the garage door, as quietly as he could.

CHAPTER 6

Norm set off, pedalling furiously down the street. Furious, not only in the sense that he was pedalling as *fast* as he possibly *could*, but mainly in the sense that by now, he'd reached the point where he was practically *oozing* anger and *fizzing* with frustration. Everything was a bit of a blur. Luckily, not *literally* a blur. Otherwise he would have most probably crashed. But it was almost as if someone else was controlling him. As if it was somehow out of his hands. Because he had no clear idea of **where** he was actually pedalling **to**. But that was fine by Norm. Pretty much **anywhere** would do, at this stage. The woods at the back of the shopping precinct, or the Amazonian rainforest. Norm didn't particularly care which. As long as the distance between **him**, his stupid little **house**, his stupid little **brothers** and **flipping** Chelsea was gradually increasing, that was **all** that mattered. And if by any chance Norm **did** find himself stranded in the middle of the Amazonian rainforest? He'd worry about that later.

Amazonian rainforest

Shopping precinct

As so often happened when Norm was riding his bike, he soon found himself lost in another world. Not some kind of **fantasy** world, with dragons and wizards and unicorns and all **that** kind of stuff – which, in **Norm's** opinion was a load of old nonsense anyway – but a world that,

90

on the surface anyway, *looked* similar to the one he already lived in, but actually *wasn't*. This was a world that revolved around *him* and him alone. A world where *he* got to call the shots and do whatever *he* wanted. *Whenever* he wanted to *do* it. A world where he was never ever blamed for stuff that he'd never ever *done*. A world where nothing was ever unfair and nothing ever annoyed him. So it might as *well* have been a fantasy world, as far as *Norm* was concerned. Because he knew it was never going to happen. Not in a *million* flipping years!

"Not stopping, then?" said a familiar-sounding voice.

Norm hadn't been *planning* to stop. At least, not for a while, anyway. But he quickly jammed on his brakes and skidded to a halt, before turning around to see the owner of the familiar sounding voice, looking at him through the allotment fence.

"Oh hi, Grandpa. Didn't realise where I was."

"Where's the fire?" said Grandpa.

"Uh?" said Norm. "What fire?"

"What's the hurry?"

"Oh, right," said Norm. "Erm, dunno really."

Grandpa frowned, his cloud-like eyebrows meeting above his nose, to form one great big cloud. "You don't *know*?"

Norm shrugged. "Not really, no."

"Kids today," said Grandpa.

Norm waited a few moments for Grandpa to finish the sentence. But it seemed that he already had.

"I'd better be off, then," said Norm eventually.

"So soon?" said Grandpa. "Aren't you going to at least ask me how I am?"

"Sorry," said Norm. "How are you, Grandpa?"

"Mustn't grumble," said Grandpa. "Where are you going, by the way?"

Norm shrugged again. "Dunno."

Grandpa **frowned** again. "Honestly?"

Norm nodded. "Honestly."

"Well, I must say, I find that rather hard to believe, Norman," said Grandpa. "Because when **I** set off somewhere, I generally have a pretty good idea where I'm going to end up. In fact, more often than not, I know **precisely** where I'm going to end up."

"Yeah, well," said Norm.

"And what's *that* supposed to mean?"

Norm shrugged *again*. "Dunno."

Grandpa regarded Norm quizzically. "Is there anything you *do* know?"

"What?" said Norm. "Yeah, loads of things."

"Such as?" said Grandpa.

"Uh?"

"Give me an example."

Norm thought for a moment. Now that he'd suddenly been put on the spot, like a contestant on a quiz show, he couldn't whink of a single thing that he knew. It was so flipping annoying. But that was before he looked up to see Grandpa's eyes crinkling ever so slightly in the corners. Which was the closest Grandpa ever came to smiling.

"I'm getting a sense of déjà vu, here, Norman."

Norm pulled a face. That was the **second** time someone had said that, today, wasn't it? Not that Norm could remember what déjà vu actually **meant**. But that wasn't the point. He just knew he'd heard it somewhere before.

"What I mean," said Grandpa, "is that this isn't the **first** time this has happened, is it?"

Whoa, spooky, thought Norm. How did Grandpa know what he'd just been thinking?

"You, cycling past here, not knowing where you are.

Not knowing where you're going?"

"Oh, right, I see," said Norm. "I dunno, Grandpa."

"You don't **know**?" said Grandpa, his eyes crinkling slightly in the corners again. "Well, **I** do!"

So why flipping **ask**, then? thought Norm, who was beginning to suspect that **everything** that had happened so far today, had happened before. And not just **once**, either. Time after flipping time. He was pretty sure he'd even had this exact same **conversation** with Grandpa before. And most **other** conversations, for that matter.

"You seem a little ..." began Grandpa, before stopping again.

A little **what**? thought Norm, who, once again, had been expecting Grandpa to actually finish the sentence, instead of leaving it hanging in mid-air like a trapeze artist at a flipping circus.

"A little ..."

"**What**, Grandpa?" said Norm.

"Distracted?" said Grandpa. "Not quite ..."

Gordon flipping **Bennet**, thought Norm as yet **again** Grandpa began a sentence but failed to **complete** it. Was this some kind of terrifying glimpse into the **future**? A sneak preview of what it was like to be **old**? Would Norm do the same thing when **he** was Grandpa's age? Start saying something and then suddenly stop, as if he'd got bored by the sound of his own voice? Not that Grandpa was **that** old, of course. He certainly didn't **act** like he was particularly **ancient**. Not like **some** people, who, as soon as they hit thirty, seemed to spend all their time moaning about the weather and the price of bread and how long they'd had to wait for a flipping bus. Not that Grandpa tried to act **younger** than he was, either. He wasn't one of those embarrassing types who wore a baseball cap back to front, or pretended to like hip hop, to try and be cool. Grandpa didn't **need** to try and be cool, as far as **Norm** was concerned. He just **was** cool. What you **saw** with Grandpa was what you **got** with Grandpa. And Norm wouldn't have it any other way.

"Not quite with it," said Grandpa finally finishing the sentence he'd started about three weeks previously. Or at least that's what it felt like to Norm.

"What do you mean, Grandpa?"

"What I **mean**," said Grandpa, "is that you've obviously got something on your mind."

"Right," said Norm.

They looked at each other for a moment.

"So are you going to tell me what it is, or am I going to have to **guess**?"

Norm sighed. Where did he **begin** to tell Grandpa what was on his mind? And if he ever **did** begin, where did he flipping **stop**? Because Norm had a

99

feeling that once he **did** begin, it would be like turning on a tap. It would all just come gushing out at once.

"How old are you, Norman?" said Grandpa, before Norm had a chance to reply. "Twelve?"

Norm nodded. "Nearly thirteen, actually."

"When's your birthday?"

"Next Saturday," said Norm, trying not to be **too** miffed that Grandpa had forgotten. Or at least, had **pretended** he'd forgotten.

"Heavens to Betsy," said Grandpa. "Who'd have thunk it?"

Uh? thought Norm. Who on earth was Betsy?

"I know what it's like, you know, Norman."

"What do you mean, Grandpa?"

"I was twelve when I was your age."

Norm couldn't help smiling. But that was the effect that Grandpa had on him. No matter how fed up he was, Grandpa could always be relied on to make him feel a bit better.

"I know what it's like to be angry all the time."

"Really?" said Norm, who couldn't imagine Grandpa ever being angry about **anything**, let alone being angry all the time.

"Well, of course," said Grandpa. "My little brothers used to drive **me** round the bend!"

"Uh?" said Norm. "You had little brothers, Grandpa?"

Grandpa nodded. "Two. Just like you."

"No one tells me anything," said Norm huffily.

"You not heard your mum talking about her uncles, then?"

"What?" said Norm. "Oh right. Yeah. Of course. I wasn't thinking."

"Makes a change," said Grandpa.

"What?" said Norm.

"Nothing," said Grandpa. "Get on with it."

Norm looked at Grandpa, as if he'd forgotten what he was supposed to be getting on with.

"Spill the beans, Norman! Spill the beans!"

"You mean ..."

"Why are you angry?" said Grandpa. "I'm all ears!"

Uh? thought Norm.

"Come on!" said Grandpa, beginning to get more and more exasperated. "I haven't got all day!"

"Really?" said Norm doubtfully. Because as far as **he** was concerned, all day was **precisely** what Grandpa had.

"Yes, **really**, Norman. These cabbages aren't going to water themselves, you know!"

Norm looked at where Grandpa had just indicated, with a tilt of his head. What was the point of going to all the trouble of actually **watering** the cabbages, when you could just wait till it rained instead? Then again, thought Norm, what was the point of **cabbages**, full flipping stop? In his opinion, eating cabbage wasn't so much a source of vitamins as a form of flipping **punishment**. He'd sooner eat flipping **cardboard** than **cabbage**. Actually, thought Norm, he'd sooner eat just about **anything** than flipping **cabbage**!

"Well?" said Grandpa.

"What?" said Norm.

"GET ON WITH IT!"

Norm sighed. "I've got to look after my brothers."

Grandpa looked at him for a few moments, but didn't say anything.

"While my mum and dad go out," Norm went on.

"And?" said Grandpa.

"And what?" said Norm.

"What else?" said Grandpa.

Norm pulled a face like a constipated koala bear. "What *else*? That's it, Grandpa!"

"Oh," said Grandpa.

Oh? thought Norm. Was that all Grandpa had

to say? *Oh*?

"For a second there, I thought it was something really ***terrible***."

"But ..." began Norm.

Grandpa shrugged. "What?"

"It ***is*** terrible, Grandpa!"

"But ..." began Grandpa.

"What?" said Norm.

"They're your ***brothers***!"

"Exactly!" said Norm.

"I'm afraid I don't understand, Norman," said Grandpa, his eyebrows knitting together again, to form another single cloud, just above his nose.

"NO ONE FLIPPING *DOES*!" wailed Norm, like a toddler on the brink of the almightiest tantrum since records began. If anyone had ever actually gone to the trouble of keeping records of tantrums in the first place, of course. Which they probably hadn't. But that wasn't the point. The point *was* that once *again*, Norm appeared to be talking in an entirely different language to everyone else on the entire flipping planet. Or that everyone else was talking in an entirely different language to *him*. But whichever way he looked at it, it still amounted to the same thing. Norm was in a world of his own. Or at least that's what it was beginning to feel like.

"Worse things happen at sea," said Grandpa.

Uh? thought Norm. And what was *that* supposed to flipping mean? Worse things happen at sea? For a *start*, Norm seriously doubted that worse things *did* happen at sea. And even if they *did*, he didn't particularly *care*.

106

"How long have you got to look after them for?" said Grandpa.

Norm shrugged. "Dunno. A couple of hours, maybe. It's **SO** unfair."

"Really?" said Grandpa.

"Yeah, **really**," said Norm.

"Well, I'm afraid I don't know what to suggest," said Grandpa.

"Wait a minute," said Norm, the seeds of an idea suddenly starting to sprout.

"What is it?"

"I don't suppose you could look after them instead, could you, Grandpa?" said Norm, hopefully.

"When are they going out?"

"They're out now."

Grandpa shook his head, ruefully. "Ah, in that case, I'm afraid I can't."

"But ..."

"Sorry, Norman. Stuff to do. Like I said before. Haven't got all day, you know."

Norm sighed dejectedly.

Grandpa suddenly frowned, as if something had just occurred to him. Which it had.

"Hang on."

"What?" said Norm.

"Did you say your mum and dad are out *now*?"

"Er, yeah," said Norm. "I did."

"So ... who's looking after your brothers, then?" said Grandpa.

"Uh? What?" said Norm distractedly.

"Who's looking after Brian and Dave at the *moment*?"

Norm shrugged. "No one."

Grandpa eyed Norm for a couple of seconds. "No one?"

"Yeah," said Norm. "No one."

"Do you really think you should be here, Norman?" said Grandpa.

Norm was confused. What did Grandpa mean? He had to be *somewhere*, didn't he? It would be weird if he *wasn't*.

"What I mean," said Grandpa, "is, don't you think you ought to be getting back, if no one's looking after your brothers right now?"

Norm thought for a moment.

"Yeah. S'pose so."

Grandpa raised his cloud-like eyebrows. "You **suppose** so?"

Norm nodded.

"Well, I **know** so, Norman."

Norm groaned like a creaky door. Much as he hated to admit it, Grandpa was probably right. In fact, never mind **probably** right. He was **definitely** right.

"Come on," said Grandpa. "Chop-chop! Off you go!"

"Aw, man," mumbled Norm, turning himself and his bike back around until they were both facing in the direction they'd only just come from.

"Chin up," said Grandpa. "Things can only get better, you know."

"Really?" said Norm.

"Of course," said Grandpa. "Apart from when they don't."

Great, thought Norm, setting off. That was *just* what he needed to flipping know.

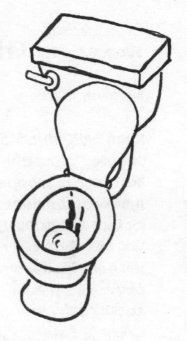

"Remember, Norman! Life is like a skid mark in a toilet bowl!"

It *is*? thought Norm, disappearing around a bend.

"SOMETIMES YOU GET PEED OFF!" yelled Grandpa at the top of his voice.

Despite everything, Norm laughed so hard, he very nearly hit a lamppost.

CHAPTER 7

Norm was still chuckling quietly to himself as he pedalled around the corner a few minutes later. But he soon stopped. Chuckling **and** pedalling. There was **someone** on his drive. And that someone looked **suspiciously** like his best friend, Mikey. Not only that, but he appeared to be talking to someone on the other side of the fence. And **that** particular someone could **only** be Chelsea. But why would **Mikey** be talking to **Chelsea?** And what could they be talking

about? Without *him*? It just didn't compute. At least, not to Norm it didn't, anyway. It wasn't long before Norm's suspicions were confirmed.

"Oh hi, Norm," said Mikey, turning around as Norm freewheeled closer.

"Hello, **Norman**!" said Chelsea.

"What are **you** doing here?" said Norm, braking to a halt.

Chelsea pulled a face. "What do you **mean**, what am I doing here, **Norman**? I **live** here, in case you'd forgotten?"

"Not **you**," said Norm, instantly irritated.

"Who? **Me**?" said Mikey.

"I don't see anyone **else** here, Mikey, do you?"

Mikey looked confused.

"You **doughnut**."

"**That's** not a very nice way to speak to your friend," said Chelsea.

"Exactly," said Norm.

Chelsea pulled a face. "What do you mean, **exactly**?"

"I mean he's **my** friend, not **yours**," said Norm. "I'll talk to him however I flipping **want** to!"

"Oooooh!" wailed Chelsea sarcastically. "Pardon me for **breathing**!"

Gordon flipping **Bennet**, thought Norm, gritting his teeth. There was only so much of this he could take. And he'd already reached his limit.

"Well?" said Chelsea.

"Well, what?" said Norm, with a shrug of his shoulders.

"Aren't you going to apologise?"

"Who to?"

"**Mikey**, of course!" said Chelsea.

"**Mikey**?" said Norm. "What for?"

"For calling him a doughnut!" said Chelsea.

"It's OK," grinned Mikey. "I don't mind."

"Well you **should** mind, Mikey," said Chelsea.

"Should I?" said Mikey.

"Definitely," said Chelsea.

"You know what **you** should mind?" said Norm, glaring venomously at Chelsea.

"What?" said Chelsea.

"Your own flipping business," said Norm.

"Ha!" said Chelsea. "That's actually quite funny."

"Uh?" said Norm in amazement. "Really?"

"Yeah," said Chelsea. "For you."

For a few moments, Norm was convinced that he was about to explode. Which, on the one hand, would be a perfect excuse not to have to look after his brothers.

But on the other hand, knowing *his* luck, he'd *still* be expected to clean up the flipping mess afterwards.

"Anyway, it's rude to interrupt," said Chelsea.

"Uh?" said Norm. "What are you on about?"

"Mikey and I were in the middle of a conversation. A *private* conversation. Weren't we, Mikey?"

"Erm, yeah. Actually we *were*, kind of, Norm," said Mikey, sheepishly.

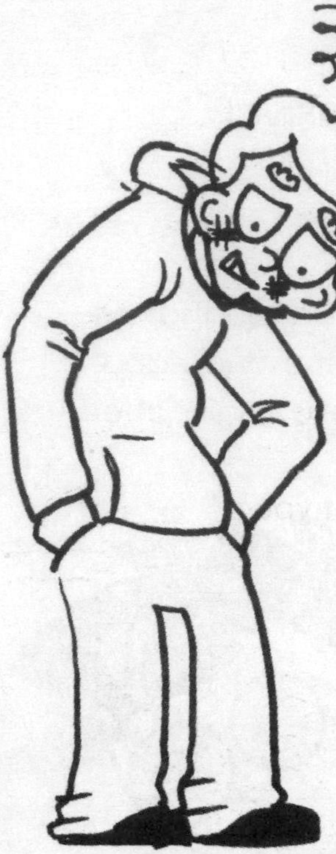

"What about?" said Norm.

"Pardon?" said Chelsea incredulously.

"What was the conversation about?" snarled Norm, rapidly running out of what little patience he'd had in the first place.

"I *told* you," said Chelsea. "It was a *private* conversation!"

"Yeah? So?" said Norm.

Chelsea frowned and tilted her head as if she couldn't quite believe what she was hearing.

"Are you *serious*?"

Norm shrugged. "Course I'm serious."

"What part of *private* do you not understand, Norman?"

118

"But ..." began Norm.

"What?" said Chelsea.

"Mikey's on my drive."

Chelsea laughed. "So?"

"*My* drive," said Norm. "Not his. Not yours."

"What's your point, caller?" said Chelsea as if she was a radio presenter talking to a listener who'd phoned up.

"What?" said Norm.

"What difference does it make, *where* we're actually having the conversation?" said Chelsea.

"It means it's not private," said Norm.

"OK," said Chelsea. "Firstly, technically it's your mum and dad's drive. Not **yours**. And secondly ..."

"Yeah?" said Norm, expectantly. "What?"

Chelsea sighed. "I don't even know where to begin. Because that's the biggest pile of panda poop I've ever heard in my life!"

"That doesn't even make sense," said Norm.

"What doesn't?" said Chelsea.

"How can you **hear** a pile of panda poop?"

"It makes more sense than what you just said, **Norman**!"

"Flipping doesn't," muttered Norm.

"Flipping **does**!"

"But ..." began Norm.

"Just because Mikey's on 'your' drive," said Chelsea, making speech marks in the air with her fingers, "doesn't mean he has to tell you what we were **talking** about!"

"Yeah, it 'does'," said Norm, making speech marks in the air with **his** fingers.

"That **definitely** doesn't make sense," laughed Chelsea.

"She's got a point, Norm," said Mikey.

Norm turned slowly and looked at his best friend, as if Mikey had just announced that he was half penguin.

"What did you just say, Mikey?"

"I said she's got a point. We don't have to tell you what we were talking about, if we don't want to."

"And **do** you want to?" said Norm.

"No, we don't," interjected Chelsea, before Mikey could reply for himself.

"Sorry, Norm," mumbled Mikey.

"Sorry for **what**?" said Chelsea. "For not **agreeing** with him?"

"I'm not sure," said Mikey.

"I don't care," said Norm nonchalantly.

"What?" said Chelsea.

"I don't want to know, anyway."

"Yeah, right," said Chelsea.

"I don't," said Norm.

"I don't believe you, **Norman**."

Norm looked at Chelsea. How was it even **possible** for one person to be so unbe-flipping-**lievably** annoying? Was she genetically **programmed** to be that way, from birth? Because of course Chelsea was right. Norm abso-flipping-**lutely** wanted to know what she and Mikey had been talking about, just before he'd turned up. Why wouldn't they say what it **was**? What was the big deal? Why all the flipping **secrecy**, all of a flipping sudden? Because all **that** did was make him want to know even **more**!

"I'll give you one more chance, Mikey."

Mikey pulled a face. "One more chance to what?"

"To tell me what you were talking about, just now," said Norm.

"But ..."

"What?" said Norm.

"I thought you said you didn't want to know."

Norm shrugged. "I don't. I just thought you might want to tell me anyway. You know? Get it off your chest and stuff."

"Nice try, **Norman**!" grinned Chelsea.

"What do you **mean**?" said Norm. Even though he knew **exactly** what Chelsea meant.

"You're so transparent!"

Uh? thought Norm. What was she on about now? **Transparent**?

"I can see right through you!"

Gordon flipping **Bennet**, thought Norm. So now Chelsea reckoned she had some kind of flipping **superpower**, did she? What did she think he **was**? **Stupid** or something? And what was the point of seeing right through someone, anyway? That would be a **rubbish** superpower. Why not just ask them to move instead? Or, better still, wait till they'd gone?

"Oh well," said Mikey, beginning to wheel his bike away. "Better get going, I suppose."

"Uh?" said Norm.

"I'd better get going, Norm." said Mikey, stopping again.

"But I've only just **got** here," said Norm.

"Yeah, I know you have," said Mikey. "But ..."

Norm shrugged. "What?"

Mikey glanced quickly at Chelsea. But not quite quickly enough.

"What did you look at **her** for, Mikey?"

"Pardon?" said Mikey.

"You heard," said Norm. "What did you look at Chelsea like that, for?"

"No reason," said Mikey. "I just did."

But that wasn't good enough, as far as Norm was concerned. Something was going on and he knew it. But what? That was the question.

"He can look at whoever he wants to look at, **Norman**," said Chelsea. "It's not a **crime**, you know."

"What?" said Norm.

"It's not actually **illegal** to look at someone else."

Norm sighed. He wished it was illegal for **Chelsea** to look at **him**. Or speak to him, for that matter. Or be anywhere **near** him. In fact, come to think of it, thought Norm, it was a pity Chelsea wasn't just generally illegal. It would make his life **so** much more bearable. Because the mere **thought** of her popping up on the other side of the fence every time he set foot out the front door was enough to bring him out in a flipping **rash**.

"Sorry, Norm," said Mikey.

"What do you keep *apologising* for, Mikey?" said Chelsea.

"Sorry," said Mikey.

"There you go again!" said Chelsea. "You've got nothing to be sorry *for*! You came here. He wasn't in. And now you're going back. End of."

Norm turned to Mikey. "Is that what happened?"

"Er, yeah," said Mikey. "Of course. That's *exactly* what happened, Norm. I came round to see if you could go biking. But you weren't in."

Norm desperately wanted to believe his best friend. But he still had his doubts.

"So you didn't come round for any *other* reason, then?"

"What?" said Mikey. "No. No other reason."

"Promise?" said Norm.

"He's already told you, hasn't he?" said Chelsea. "What's the big deal?"

Yeah, thought Norm. Much as it pained him to **agree** with Chelsea about something. Or anything, for that matter. What **was** the big deal? He wished he knew. All he knew was that it somehow **was** a big deal. Well, at least to **Norm** it was, anyway.

"Sorry, Norm," said Mikey.

"Stop that!" said Chelsea.

"Why have you still got to go, Mikey?" said Norm. "I'm here **now**."

"HE JUST HAS!" yelled Chelsea. "GET OVER IT!"

Gordon flipping **Bennet**, thought Norm. He wished that he **could** get over it. But that was easier said than flipping done. Because there was **still** something niggling away at the back of his mind, like a wasp continually bashing itself against a window, desperately trying to get out.

"What about later on, then?" said Norm.

"What about it?" said Mikey.

"Can you go biking?" said Norm.

"Erm ..." began Mikey hesitantly.

"No, he **can't**," said Chelsea. "He's got stuff on already. Haven't you, Mikey?"

"What?" said Mikey. "Erm, I mean, yeah. I have."

"Stuff?" said Norm, suspiciously. "What **kind** of stuff?"

"Oh, just, you know … stuff stuff?" said Mikey.

"Stuff stuff?" said Norm.

Mikey nodded.

"Right. Well, I'm glad we've cleared that up," said Chelsea. "I suppose I'd better be off, too."

"So soon?" muttered Norm.

"What was that, **Norman**?" said Chelsea.

"Nothing," said Norm.

"Good," said Chelsea, disappearing. "Hasta luego, Mikey."

"Yeah, see you later," said Mikey.

Norm turned and looked at Mikey for a few seconds. Or rather, Norm turned and **glared** at Mikey for a few seconds.

"What's up, Norm?" said Mikey.

"You said 'see you later'."

"Did I?"

"Yeah, you did," said Norm. "To Chelsea."

Mikey shrugged. "It's just a figure of speech."

"Really?"

"Yeah, of course," said Mikey. "Like 'see you soon', or 'see you around.'"

"Hmmm," said Norm, still not convinced. "So just because you **said** it, doesn't necessarily mean you actually **are** going to see her later on, then?"

"Not necessarily, no."

Norm glared at Mikey for a few more seconds.

"Mikey?"

"Yeah?" said Mikey.

"**Are** you going to see Chelsea, later, or not?"

Mikey shrugged again. "Dunno. Maybe."

Norm huffed and puffed like an old steam train. "Gordon flipping **Bennet**, Mikey! What do you mean, '**maybe**'?"

"I mean I don't **know**!" said Mikey

starting to get quite agitated himself. "I might."

"You **might**?"

"Yeah, well I mean, who **knows** what's going to happen in the future, Norm?"

Norm sighed. "Gordon flipping **Bennet**!"

"Sorry, but I've really got to go now, Norm!"

Norm watched as his best friend got on his bike and rode off down the street.

"Oh, **there** you are!" said a voice. "We were **wondering** where you'd got to."

Norm swivelled around to see not only Brian, standing in the front doorway, but Dave, too.

"What's on the menu?" said Dave.

"Uh?" said Norm.

"For lunch?" said Brian.

Norm groaned, like an old man getting up from a chair. His brothers were *so* flipping annoying. Even *more* annoying than *Chelsea*. And *that* was flipping saying something.

CHAPTER 8

The big question, as far as **Norm** was concerned, wasn't what was on the menu for lunch that particular day. The big question, as far as **Norm** was concerned, was did his brothers actually **realise** they'd been left home alone, whilst **he'd** been out and about on his bike? Or had they been so engrossed in the Xbox that they hadn't even noticed he'd gone? And anyway, thought Norm, there **wasn't** a flipping menu for lunch. Or any other meal, for that matter. Who did they think he was? Some kind of flipping **servant**? Honestly. Kids today.

"I was just riding around on the drive," said Norm, following Brian and Dave into the kitchen.

"Right," said Brian.

"Yeah. Just practising a few wheelies and track stands and stuff."

"So?" said Brian.

"So, I was definitely wasn't anywhere else," said Norm.

"Pardon?" said Brian.

"I didn't go anywhere else. Just stayed on the drive."

"OK," said Brian.

"You know? Just in case you were thinking that I *did* go anywhere else?" said Norm. "I was definitely here all the time."

"I should think so too," said Brian. "Because you're supposed to be looking after us."

"Yeah, I know," said Norm.

"Well then?" said Brian. "Why would you be somewhere else, if you were supposed to be looking after us? I don't understand."

Gordon flipping **Bennet**, thought Norm, beginning to wish he hadn't bothered saying anything. Because all he seemed to be doing was digging himself deeper and deeper into trouble. And trouble was the last thing he wanted. Well, maybe not the last thing he wanted. But definitely **one** of the last things.

"Yeah, Norman," grinned Dave.

"What?" said Norm.

"Why **would** you be somewhere else?"

"What are you on about, Dave?" said Norm.

"Nothing," said Dave angelically. "Just wondered, that's all."

Norm eyeballed his youngest brother for a moment. For a seven-year-old, Dave could be remarkably perceptive at times. As well as **incredibly** irritating, of course. That went without saying. Or thinking, anyway. **Both** his brothers could be incredibly irritating. They always flipping **had** been and no doubt they always flipping **would** be. It was as if it was their actual **job** to be incredibly irritating and make his life as miserable as possible. But whereas **Brian** never ever **stopped** being irritating, just occasionally, Norm caught a glimpse of a different

Dave. Or at least, he caught a glimpse of another **side** of Dave. And what Norm saw, on those occasional occasions, was a pretty smart cookie. Not that Norm was any kind of expert when it came to the average intelligence of cookies. But he knew that this was most definitely one of those occasions. Because Norm somehow **knew** that **Dave** somehow knew that he'd been out. He could just tell by the way Dave had looked at him. And not only that but Norm was pretty sure that Dave **knew** he knew he knew he'd been out. But that wasn't the point. The point **was**: when would Dave use this information to his advantage? Because he was **bound** to sooner or later. Not that Norm could blame him if he **did**. Because if it had been the other way round, **he**

would have done exactly the same thing. "So?" said Brian.

"What?" said Norm distractedly.

"What *is* for lunch, then?" said Brian.

Norm shrugged. "I dunno. What are you asking *me* for?"

Brian looked at Norm for a second or two. "Isn't it obvious?"

Uh? thought Norm. Well of *course* it wasn't flipping obvious. Otherwise he wouldn't be flipping *asking*, would he?

"No?" said Brian.

No, *what*? thought Norm, starting to simmer, like a saucepan of soup. And if Brian didn't hurry up and

get on with it, he was going to flipping well boil over.

"You don't honestly expect us to get our own **lunch**, do you?" said Brian.

Norm pulled a face. "What?"

"I said, you don't honestly expect us to get our own lunch, do you?"

"No, I **heard** you," said Norm. "I just ..."

"Just what?" said Brian.

"Is this some kind of wind-up, Brian?" said Norm. "It is, isn't it?"

"What do you mean, wind-up?" said Brian, completely straight-faced.

"You're actually **serious**?" said Norm. "You're honestly expecting **me** to make lunch for you?"

"Well of course we are!" said Brian. "Who else is going to make it?"

"Er, **Mum**?" said Norm. "Obviously."

"**Not** obviously," said Dave.

"What did you say, Dave?" said Norm.

"That's **sexist**, that is."

"What are you **talking** about?" said Norm, as if Dave had suddenly started talking in Mandarin.

"Expecting **Mum** to make lunch," said Dave. "That's *sexist*."

"Shut up, Dave, you little freak!" hissed Norm.

"Charming," said Dave.

"It *is* actually a bit sexist though, Norman," said Brian.

"A *bit*?" said Dave in astonishment. "It's *very* sexist, actually. Dads can cook too, you know."

"Ours can't," said Brian.

"What?" said Dave.

"Our dad can't cook," said Brian. "He's a rubbish cook."

"True," said Dave.

"But that's not the point," said Brian. "The point is ..."

"You can shut up as well, Brian," said Norm. "*That's*

144

what the flipping point is."

"Language," said Dave.

"What?" said Norm.

"I'm telling," said Brian.

"Telling **what**?" said Norm. "That I was out on my **bike**?"

The kitchen suddenly fell silent, as if someone had hit the mute button. Straight away, Norm realised

he'd just made a big mistake. But exactly **how** big? He had a funny feeling he was about to find out.

"Pardon?" said Brian.

"Er, nothing," said Norm.

"You think I'm going to **tell**, because you were out on **your** bike?"

"Erm …"

"I was **going** to tell because you **swore**," said Brian.

"Oh, right," said Norm.

"And anyway, you were only out on the **drive**," said Dave mischievously. "**Weren't** you, Norman?"

"What?" said Norm.

"Well I mean it's not as if you went anywhere **else**, on your bike, is **it**?" said Dave, with a knowing wink. A knowing wink which, luckily, only **Norm** could see.

"Oh, right," said Norm, finally twigging. "No, course not."

"So there's no reason why Brian would tell Mum and Dad about *that* then, is there?"

"Er, no. Don't suppose there is," said Norm.

"Well then," said Dave.

Well then indeed, thought Norm. Even though in his opinion, *flipping* wasn't even a swear word. Not a proper flipping swear word, anyway. Flipping cheek, Brian even suggesting that it *was*. On the *other* hand, thank goodness Dave had stepped in to save the day when he did. Before Brian had realised what was going on.

"Anyway, Mum's not here at the moment, is she?" said Dave. "Or Dad."

"Doesn't matter," said Brian. "I'll tell them later."

147

Yeah, thought Norm. Knowing **Brian**, he probably **would** flipping tell his mum and dad later. In fact, knowing **Brian**, he'd probably make a flipping **appointment** with his mum and dad, **specifically** to tell them later. **That's** how unbe-flipping-lievably annoying **he** was.

"No, I meant they're not here to make lunch for us," said Dave.

"Oh, right," said Brian. "Good point."

"Well don't look at **me**," said Norm.

But it was too late. Brian and Dave were **already** looking at Norm. And they weren't the only ones, either.

"WOOF!" went John, padding into the kitchen.

"What's that, John?" said Brian. "**You** want to know what's for lunch, **too**?"

Norm sighed. "***Seriously***, Brian?"

"What do you mean?" said Brian. "I hope you're not suggesting that I can't understand what John's saying?"

"Gordon flipping ***Bennet***!" said Norm. "He's not saying ***anything,*** Brian, you ***idiot***! He's a flipping ***dog***. And that's not a swear word, by the way. So don't even flipping ***think*** about it!"

"WOOF!" went John, again.

149

"What's that, John?" said Norm. "You think we should phone for a *pizza*?"

"Now you're just being *silly*, Norman," said Brian.

"Oh yeah?" said Norm. "Well you're just being a ... a ... a ..."

"A *what*?" said Brian.

"A ... bumhead," said Norm.

Brian pulled a face. "A *bumhead*? What *are* you? *Three*, or something?"

"Actually, that's not a bad idea," said Dave.

Norm and Brian turned towards their youngest brother.

"Actually that's a very *good* idea," said Dave.

"What is?" said Norm.

"To phone up for a pizza."

Come to think of it, thought Norm, it **was** a very good idea. And not only that, but **he'd** thought of it. The only surprise, was how come he hadn't thought of it **before**?! But that wasn't the point. The point was, now he **had** thought of it, how were they actually going to **do** it? Not the phoning up bit. That was easy. The actual **paying** for it bit. That might prove to be somewhat trickier.

"I know what you're **thinking**, Norman," said Dave.

Norm pulled a face. "Really?"

"Not **all** the time, obviously," said Dave. "That would be weird. I mean I know what you're thinking right **now**."

"Oh, right," said Norm. "So what **am** I thinking right now, Dave?"

"You're thinking, if we **do** phone for a pizza, how are we going to **pay** for it?"

Whoa, thought Norm. Dave was *good*. Not only **perceptive**, but psychic, too.

"Well?" said Dave. "Are you? Or were you?"

"Yeah, I was, actually" said Norm. "Why? Have you got any ideas?"

"As a matter of fact, I do," said Dave.

"Well?" said Norm, expectantly. "Spill the beans."

"WOOF!" went John.

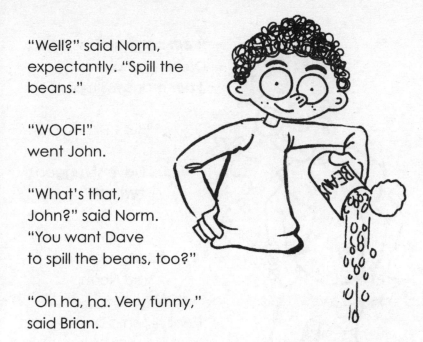

"What's that, John?" said Norm. "You want Dave to spill the beans, too?"

"Oh ha, ha. Very funny," said Brian.

"We pay using **your** money, Norman."

Brilliant, thought Norm. Why hadn't **he** thought of that? There was just one **teensy** little problem. He didn't actually **have** any money. He was skint. Flat broke. Not a single **penny** to his name, let alone a flipping **pound**. Apart from **that** though, it was a **fantastic** idea.

"No, but **seriously**, Dave."

"I **am** being serious," said Dave. "We pay using **your** money. Simple."

"But ..."

Dave shrugged. "What?"

"I don't actually **have** any money," said Norm.

"Really?" said Dave.

Norm nodded. "Really."

"Oh, that **is** a shame."

A **shame**? thought Norm. It was a flipping **disaster**, that's what it was!

"Unless ..." began Dave, before tailing off again.

Unless **what**? thought Norm. Unless he suddenly won the lottery? Because there was just one teensy little problem with *that*, too. He didn't actually *do* the flipping lottery! Of course, there was another option. He could rob a bank. Well, except that if he did, Brian would probably tell his parents. So, thinking about it, that was *another* no-no.

"I could lend you the money," said Dave.

"Pardon?" said Norm.

"I could lend *you* the money. *You* pay for the pizza – and then pay me back."

Norm thought about this for a moment. And the reason he only thought about it for a *moment*, was because he knew that if he thought about it for much *longer*, his brain would start to bubble and melt, like grilled cheese on toast.

"Wait a minute," said Brian. "So **you** lend the money to **Norman**. **Norman** buys the pizza and then pays you back afterwards?"

"Exactly," said Dave.

"But ..."

"But what?" said Dave.

"Why don't **you** just pay for the pizza?" said Brian. "And then Mum and Dad pay you back, when they get home?"

It was a good point, thought Norm. Why **didn't** Dave just pay for the pizza? Surely that would be **much** simpler. And much cheaper for Norm, too.

"I think **Norman** knows," said Dave. "**Don't** you, Norman?"

Norm looked confused. "I do?"

"He owes me one."

Brian looked confused, too. "Norman owes you a *pizza*?"

Dave winked. But once again, it was a wink which Norm, and Norm alone, could see. And suddenly Norm, and Norm alone, knew **precisely** why he owed Dave a pizza. Or at least, why Dave might **think** he did, anyway.

"Oh, yeah," said Norm, through gritted teeth. "I do. I remember now."

"Norman?" said Brian.

"What?" said Norm.

"What's that ... *thing* on the side of your head?"

Thing? thought Norm, his mind immediately going into overdrive. What *kind* of thing?

"It's just a vein," said Dave. "It's throbbing, that's all."

That's *all*? thought Norm. The way his brothers were going on, made it sound like his head was about to *explode*!

"Oh yeah," said Brian. "Like Dad's does, you mean?"

"Yeah," said Dave. "Exactly."

"What do you *mean*, like *Dad's* does?" said Norm. "What are you two *on* about?"

"The vein on the side of Dad's head that starts to throb when he gets stressed?" said Dave.

"Dad's head throbs when he gets stressed?" said Norm.

"No!" laughed Brian. "Not his whole **head**! Just the **vein**! Have you never noticed, Norman?"

"No," said Norm. Which was true. He never **had** noticed. Then again, there were some days when Norm wouldn't notice if he stepped outside and it was raining gerbils.

"So?" said Dave. "What do you **think**?"

Norm pulled a face. What did he think about what? Or what did he think, in general? Because if so, that could take some time.

"I lend you the money so that you can pay for the pizza?" said Dave.

"Oh, right," said Norm. "But ..."

"What?" said Dave.

"How do I pay you back?"

Dave smiled. "That's **your** problem, isn't it, Norman?"

"Perhaps you'll get some money for your birthday?" said Brian.

"Seriously?" said Norm. "Who from?"

"Mum and Dad?"

Norm sighed. He'd be lucky to get a flipping **card** from his mum and dad, never mind flipping **money**. But Dave was right. It was his problem. Because one thing was certain.

Now that they'd **mentioned** getting a pizza, they were definitely going to have to do it. It would be a form of mental torture **not** to. Like standing in front of a toilet and not being allowed to pee. Well, maybe

not *quite* like that, thought Norm. But that wasn't the point. The point was, if it meant borrowing money from **Dave**, in order to actually **buy** the pizza, then that was precisely what he was going to have to do. He'd figure out a way of paying Dave back, sooner or later. Preferably later.

"Well?" said Dave.

Norm nodded. "'Kay. Whatever."

"Excellent!" said Dave. "How does a sixteen-inch, thick crust Margherita sound?"

It sounded abso-flipping-lutely **brilliant**, thought Norm. And it would **taste** even better!

"WOOF!" went John.

"What's that, John?" said Brian. "You'd like potato wedges

and a portion of garlic bread with that?"

Gordon flipping **Bennet**, thought Norm, heading for the phone.

CHAPTER 9

"How long?" said Brian, when Norm eventually wandered back into the kitchen.

Until what? thought Norm. The **COWS** came home?

"Till the pizza's here?" said Brian, sensing his older brother's confusion.

"Oh, right," said Norm. "About ten minutes."

Brian looked horrified. "*Ten* minutes? *Seriously*?"

Norm sighed. "No. Sorry, Brian. My mistake. I meant ten *seconds*."

"Whoa!" said Brian. "Really?"

"No," said Norm. "Not really."

"Oh, I see," said Brian. "You were being sarcastic."

"You *think*?" said Norm, sarcastically.

"You know what they say, don't you, Norman?"

"Know what *who* say?"

"I don't know," said Brian with a shrug. "The people who say stuff, I suppose."

Gordon flipping *Bennet*, thought Norm. Was it just *him*, or was Brian being even *more* annoying than usual? Because it was almost as if he'd walked out of *one* world to make a phone call and walked back into an entirely **different** world. A world which Norm didn't even **begin** to understand.

"So, what **do** they say then, Brian?" prompted Dave. "These people that say stuff?"

"What?" said Brian. "Oh, right. Yeah. They say that sarcasm is the lowest form of humour."

Hang on, thought Norm. He'd had this conversation **before**, hadn't he? Not today, obviously. But he'd **definitely** had it before. Possibly on **more** than one occasion. Along with all the **other** conversations he'd had before on more than one occasion. At least that's what it felt like. And it was beginning to get pretty flipping annoying.

"Wikipizza?" said Dave.

"What?" said Norm distractedly.

"Did you order from Wikipizza?"

Norm looked at Dave as if Dave had just asked whether he'd put his pants on the right way round, or not. Because in terms of stupid questions, this was right up there with the very **stupidest**. Had he ordered from **Wikipizza**? Of course he'd ordered from Wikipizza! Times might have been hard. But they weren't that flipping hard. A guy had his limits. And in **Norm's** case, that meant eating any kind of pizza that was inferior to Wikipizza pizza. Which in **Norm's** opinion meant virtually **every** other kind of pizza in the known universe. Not that Norm **had** tried every other kind of pizza in the known universe.

Unfortunately. But nothing he had tried had ever come even remotely close to Wikipizza. And probably never would, either.

"Well?" said Dave. "Did you?"

Norm sighed wearily. "Yes, Dave. I did."

"Good."

Despite everything, Norm still couldn't help chuckling. Dave might be a devious little doughnut, but at least he had decent taste.

"What are you laughing at?" said Brian.

"None of your flipping *business*, Brian," said Norm. "I just am, right?"

"All right, calm down," said Brian. "I was just *asking*."

"Yeah, well, don't," said Norm.

"Who rattled *his* cage?" whispered Brian, to Dave. But not quite quietly enough.

"What flipping cage?" snapped Norm, like a crotchety crocodile. "What are you *on* about?"

"Nothing," said Brian quickly.

"I'm warning you, Bri ..." began Norm, before suddenly stopping mid-sentence and gazing up at the ceiling.

"What's **wrong**?" said Dave.

"Uh?" said Norm. "What's wrong?"

"Yeah."

"What do **you** think, Dave?"

"I've got no idea," said Dave, who, in fairness, **did** genuinely **look** as if he had no idea what Norm might be referring to.

"Who turned the light on?"

"Pardon?" said Dave.

"You heard," said Norm. "Which one of you little freaks of nature turned the flipping **light** on while I was ordering the pizza?"

Brian and Dave glanced at each other. Clearly one of them had. The light hadn't suddenly switched *itself* on, in Norm's absence.

"Er, I did," said Brian hesitantly.

"Why?" said Norm.

"I don't know," said Brian. "I just did."

"You just *did*?" said Norm, as if he couldn't believe what he was hearing.

"Yeah," said Brian. "What's wrong with that?"

"It's the middle of the flipping *day*, Brian!" said Norm. "*That's* what's wrong with it!"

"But ..."

"No buts, Brian," said Norm. "It's a complete waste of electricity!"

"But ..."

"I said no more buts! Turn it off again. **Now**!"

Brian pulled a face. "Why?"

"Because I flipping say so and that's all there is to it!" yelled Norm. "And don't answer back!"

"All right, all right," muttered Brian as he skipped to the doorway and switched the light off. "You're beginning to sound like Dad."

Norm turned around to find Dave staring at him.

"What are **you** looking at?"

"Are you **OK**, Norman?"

"What do you mean, am I OK?"

"Well, you're acting all weird."

Norm thought for a moment. Dave was right. He **was** acting all weird. Not like, full-on, running through the shopping precinct dressed as **Spiderman** weird. But even so, **something** was most definitely going on. Because he wouldn't **normally** be bothered by anything as trivial or as boring as a flipping **light** being switched on when it shouldn't

be. He couldn't **normally** care **less** about wasting flipping electricity. Quite the opposite. The more electricity he wasted, the flipping better, as far as

Norm was concerned. So, what was happening? Because the sort of things that were beginning to wind him up were the sort of things that old people got wound up about. Old people like ...

"Norman?" said Dave anxiously.

Gordon flipping **Bennet**, thought Norm as it suddenly hit him like a tonne of wet fish. What had Brian just said? That he was beginning to sound like his **dad**? What with that and the flipping vein on the side of his head, throbbing, could it be that he was actually turning into his dad? Not literally turning **into** his dad, like in some stupid fairy tale. But starting to act and **behave** like him? No, please, thought Norm. Anything but **that**. Never

173

mind **fairy tale**. That would be more like a flipping **horror movie**.

"What's the matter?" grinned Brian. "You look like you've just seen a ghost!"

A **ghost**? thought Norm. It was worse than that. **Much** worse than that. What he'd just seen was a nightmarish vision of the future. A future which might have already begun.

"Which day's your birthday, Norman?" said Dave. "Next Saturday?"

"Uh?" said Norm, snapping out of it. "Er, yeah. Why?"

"And you're going to be thirteen, right?"

Norm shrugged. "Yeah, but ..."

"That explains it, then," said Dave, as if it was the simplest thing in the world.

"Explains **what**?" said Norm.

"You've got raging hormones," said Dave.

"Aw, yuk, that's **disgusting**!" said Brian, pulling a face as if he'd just sucked on a piece of lemon.

"No, it's **not**, Brian," said Dave. "We've all got them."

"We've all got raging hormones?" said Brian.

"Well, we haven't all got **raging** hormones. But we've all got **hormones**. It's perfectly natural."

Norm looked at his little brother in amazement. How did he even **know** this stuff? Raging Hormones sounded more like the name of a band to him.

"Really?" said Brian.

Dave nodded. "They control your moods and the way you feel and stuff."

"Cool," said Brian.

"Yeah," said Dave. "Except sometimes they go a bit bonkers."

"Whoa," said Brian.

"Want to talk about it, Norman?" said Dave.

Norm pulled a face. "Seriously, Dave? Do I want to talk about my **hormones**?"

"Yeah," said Dave.

"No," said Norm. "As a matter of flipping fact, I **don't**."

Dave smiled, knowingly. "Oh, I see."

And what was **that** supposed to mean? wondered Norm. What exactly did Dave see?

"I think you're in denial."

"WHAAAAT?" squawked Norm in disbelief. Because this really was getting too much. In fact never mind **getting** too much, thought Norm. It was too much already.

"You're in **denial**," said Dave. "It means you're refusing to accept that something is true."

"Oh yeah?" said Norm. "Well, you're ... you're ... you're ..."

"I'm what?" said Dave.

"Going to get a boot up the bum if you're not careful," said Norm.

"Oh, well, that's **very** mature, isn't it?" said Dave.

"Dave?" said Brian.

"Yes?" said Dave.

"Is Norman in denial because he's got raging hormones?"

"I'm not sure," said Dave. "Possibly."

Brian nodded. "Right."

"GORDON FLIPPING BENNET!" yelled Norm at the top of his voice. "I'm still here, you know! You're not watching some flipping *documentary* on TV!"

Brian laughed.

"Seriously though," said Dave. "Thirteen, eh? That's pretty old!"

"Shut up, Dave!" said Norm.

"Hey, it's OK," said Dave. "**None** of us are getting any younger."

"Be pretty weird if we were," said Brian.

Norm sighed. Partly because he was beginning to wonder just how much more of this he could take before he literally flipped his flipping lid. But **mainly** because maybe – just **maybe** – Dave had struck a bit of a nerve. Maybe Norm really **was** getting old. Well, of course he was getting **old**. Or **older**, anyway. Brian was right. It would be weird if he wasn't. But maybe there was a grain of truth

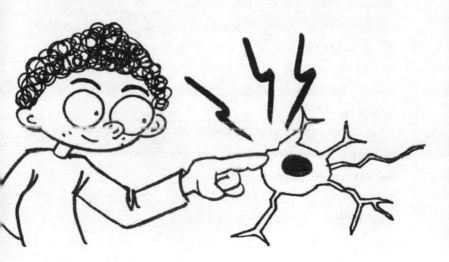

in some of the other things Dave was saying. About hormones and stuff? Even though it **was** pretty gross. But in a way, Norm almost hoped that it was his hormones that were making him act so strangely. Because the thought that he might actually be turning into his dad, really was too horrible to think about. So for now, thought Norm, he was going to do his best not to think about it.

"WOOF!" went John.

"What's that, John?" said Brian. "There's someone at the door?"

"Uh?" said Norm irritably. "How do you know that's what he—"

"Shhhh!" said Brian holding up a finger. "Three ... two ... one ... and ..."

Right on cue, the doorbell rang.

"Clever boy," said Brian in a funny squeaky voice, whilst bending down and giving John a pat on the back. "Yes, you *are*, aren't you? Yes, you *are*! You're a good boy!"

"Well?" said Dave, to Norm.

"Well, what?" said Norm, still a bit miffed that Brian had been right. Or rather, that *John* had been right.

"That'll be the pizza."

"Oh, right. Yeah."

"Well?" said Dave, again, after a couple of seconds.

"Well, what?" said Norm, again.

"Aren't you going to go and get it?"

Norm shrugged. "Why should *I* get it?"

"Because I'm going to go and get the money," said Dave, heading for the stairs.

"Uh?" said Norm.

"So that you can pay for it?"

"Oh, right, yeah," said Norm. "Forgot."

The doorbell rang, again.

"All right, all right!" yelled Norm, trudging towards the front door. "Keep your flipping hair on!"

CHAPTER 10

The *first* thing that Norm noticed, when he opened the front door, was that there *wasn't* a pizza delivery guy standing on the other side of it. The *second* thing he noticed was that *Grandpa* was standing on the other side of it. The *third* thing Norm noticed was that Grandpa *was* actually holding a pizza box. And crucially, not just *any* old pizza box, either. A *Wikipizza* box. So, thinking about it, thought Norm thinking about it, it *was* a pizza delivery guy after all. Just not the pizza delivery guy he'd been expecting.

"Ta da," said Grandpa, flatly and without the slightest trace of excitement in his voice.

"Hi, Grandpa," said Norm.

"I heard that, by the way."

Weird, thought Norm. Why would Grandpa tell him that he'd heard what he'd only just **said**?

"Keep your hair on?"

Norm pulled a face. "Sorry, what?"

"As you were coming to the door?" said Grandpa. "You said, 'keep your hair on'."

"Oh, right," said Norm, finally twigging what Grandpa was talking about.

"Actually, what you said was, 'keep your **flipping** hair on'."

"Sorry about that, Grandpa."

"Too late," said Grandpa.

"To say sorry?" said Norm.

"No," said Grandpa, his eyes crinkling slightly in the corners. "To keep my hair on."

"Yeah," chuckled Norm. "Suppose it is."

They looked at each other for a few seconds.

"You'd better come in," said Norm, eventually. "Don't want to let the heat out, do we?"

"Doing your bit to save the planet, eh?" said Grandpa, stepping inside the house.

"What?" said Norm.

"Since when have **you** been bothered about letting the heat out?"

It was a good point, thought Norm, closing the front door again. Since when **had** he been bothered about letting the **heat** out? Or switching lights off, for that matter! Since flipping **never**, that was when! As for saving the planet? He couldn't give a flying frog about saving the flipping planet! At least, not **normally** he couldn't, anyway. So, what was going on? What was happening to him? Could it **really** be something to do with his **hormones**? Because if so, that was abso-fli—

"YEAH! GRANDPA!" shrieked Brian, bursting into the hall before Norm had the chance to finish thinking the thought that he'd been thinking. Which, thinking about it, was probably just as well.

"YEAH! GRANDPA!" screeched Dave, from the bottom of the stairs.

"Hello, you two," said Grandpa.

"WOOF!" went John, trotting out of the kitchen.

"My apologies," said Grandpa. "Hello, you **three**."

"Wait a minute," said Dave, suddenly noticing what Grandpa was holding. "Is that ..."

"Is that what?" said Grandpa.

"A **pizza**?" said Dave.

"Course it's a flipping **pizza**, Dave! You **doughnut**!" said Norm. "What else could it be?"

Brian thought for a
moment. "A Frisbee?"

"What?" said Norm.

"Could be a Frisbee,
disguised as a
pizza?" said Brian.

"That's a
coincidence," said
Dave. "We just ordered
one."

Brian looked confused.
"A Frisbee?"

"No!" said Norm. "A **_pizza_**, you idiot!"

"It's no coincidence," said Grandpa. "This is the
one that you ordered. I met him outside."

"Met **_who_** outside?" said Dave.

"The pizza delivery guy," said Grandpa. "Who do
you **_think_** I meant? Bobby Smith?"

"Who's Bobby Smith?" said Norm.

"Oh, just some guy I used to know, back in the day," said Grandpa. "Rode a motorbike. Moved to Australia. Haven't seen him for years."

"So why would *he* have been outside, then?" said Norm.

"No reason," said Grandpa. "He was just the first person I thought of."

Gordon flipping **Bennet**, thought Norm. Either he'd nodded off for a couple of minutes and missed a whole chunk of this conversation, or the world had suddenly gone stark raving mad. Either way, this was making about as much sense as an instruction manual for a washing machine, written in Bulgarian.

"Did you pay for it?" said Dave.

"Did I pay for the pizza?"

Dave nodded.

"No," said Grandpa. "I stole it."

"Whoa!" said Brian. "Like Robin Hood?"

Norm sighed. He didn't know **much** about history, but he was reasonably sure that Robin Hood hadn't become famous by stealing pizzas.

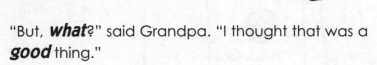

"Of **course** I paid for it."

"But ..." blurted Dave.

"But, **what**?" said Grandpa. "I thought that was a **good** thing."

"What?" said Dave. "No, it's a **brilliant** thing, Grandpa! Thanks."

"Don't mention it."

"It's just that, well, **Norman** was supposed to be paying for it!"

"Oh, **was** he now?" said Grandpa, turning to Norm.

"What?" said Norm. "Er, yeah. I was."

"You still **can**, if you really **want** to, Norman."

"What?" said Norm. "Erm ..."

"I'm just teasing," said Grandpa, his eyes crinkling slightly in the corners. "It's my treat."

"But ..." began Dave, again.

"No, really, I insist," said Grandpa. "I just had a little flutter."

Brian immediately looked concerned. "Do you want to sit down, Grandpa?"

"Pardon?" said Grandpa.

"I can get you a glass of water, if you like?"

"Not **that** kind of flutter," said Grandpa, his eyes crinkling again. "A flutter on the gee-gees!"

Norm and his brothers looked blankly at Grandpa.

"The **horses**!" said Grandpa. "I put some money on a **horse**."

Brian pulled a face. "You put some **money** on a **horse**?"

"What?" said Grandpa. "No, not *literally*, you numpty! I mean I placed a *bet* on a horse. And I won."

Ah, thought Norm. So *that* was why Grandpa couldn't come round, earlier on, when he'd asked him to. He was going to the *bookies*.

"Oh, I see," said Brian. "So you got some *money*."

Grandpa sighed. "Honestly. Don't they teach kids *anything* at school, these days?"

Norm thought for a moment. It was probably a good job that they *didn't* teach that *particular* kind of thing, at school. After all, if his dad hadn't had a so-called *little flutter* at his last job, he might still actually *have* a flipping job, *now*. And if his dad still had a job *now*, they would never have had to move to this glorified rabbit hutch and eat supermarket own-brand flipping Coco Pops!

"S'not fair," grumbled Dave.

"What isn't?" said Grandpa.

"Nothing," said Dave, looking daggers at Norm. But Norm just grinned straight back at him. He

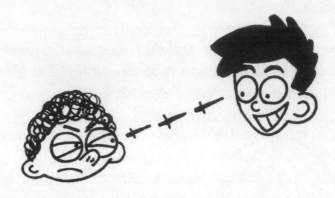

couldn't help it. Not actually having to pay for the pizza after all was the first stroke of luck he'd had all day. And knowing *his* luck, thought Norm, it would be the flipping *last* one, too. So, he might as well grab the chance to gloat, while he still could.

"Well?" said Grandpa, heading for the kitchen.

"What?" said Norm.

"Are you boys coming, or what?"

"Coming, Grandpa!" sang Brian and Dave, setting off.

194

"Excellent," said Grandpa. "Because this pizza's not going to eat itself, you know."

It was a good point, thought Norm, following his brothers. The pizza **wasn't** going to eat itself. At least, he flipping **hoped** it wasn't, anyway. And if it **did**, then he really **was** living in some kind of nightmarish vision of the future. Which reminded Norm. Whatever happened, the one thing he **mustn't** do was bang on about recycling the pizza box afterwards. Because that would prove once and for all that he really was turning into his dad! And talking about recycling, thought Norm. Or rather, talking about **cycling** ...

"Erm, Grandpa?" said Norm.

"What is it, now?" said Grandpa.

"Are you going to be here for long?"

"Who knows?" said Grandpa, mysteriously.

"Pardon?"

"Who knows how long **any** of us are going to be here?" said Grandpa. "It's impossible to say."

Gordon flipping **Bennet**, thought Norm. It was a straightforward enough question. Why couldn't he just give a straightforward **answer**?

"Er, Grandpa?" said Dave.

"Yes?" said Grandpa.

"I think Norman meant, how long are you actually going to be here, **today**? Not, when are you going to **die**?"

Brian gasped in horror.

Grandpa turned to Norm. "Did you?"

Norm nodded.

"You should have said."

Yeah, thought Norm. He flipping should have.

"Half an hour or so?" said Grandpa.

"In that case, mind if I go out on my bike for a bit?" said Norm.

"Hmmm," said Grandpa stroking his chin. "Let me think about that for a minute."

No, *please*, thought Norm. Not a whole *minute*. They'd wasted more than enough time already, having this ridiculous conversation.

"Go for it," said Grandpa, his eyes crinkling in the corners.

Norm didn't need telling twice. He went for it.

CHAPTER 11

It was only **after** Norm had set off down the road, that he realised he **still** hadn't had anything to eat, yet. Not only **that**, but the unthinkable had just happened. He'd actually set off, **without** having had any pizza. Put quite simply, this had never **ever** happened before, in all of Norm's nearly thirteen years on Planet Earth. It had **never**, as far as Norm was aware, even come close to happening. It was traumatic enough just **thinking** about it. But such was Norm's overwhelming desire to get back out on his bike again as soon as possible, that for once, he was prepared to make the ultimate sacrifice. And as far as Norm was concerned, it really was a sacrifice. After all, it wasn't just **any** old pizza he hadn't just eaten. It was a **Wikipizza** pizza that he hadn't just eaten. And a Wikipizza pizza was the food of gods.

But there could be no turning back now. Or even hesitating. Because the longer Norm was out, the more chance there was of his mum and dad coming home and discovering that he wasn't there. And OK, so technically, **Grandpa** was looking after Brian and Dave now. It wasn't like Norm had simply abandoned his brothers and left them to their own electronic devices. Much as he would have **liked** to. But even so, Norm didn't want to give his parents even the slightest **glimmer** of a reason to make him stay inside for a fraction of a second longer than he abso-flipping-lutely **had** to.

And knowing them, thought Norm, they flipping well would find the slightest glimmer of a reason. Because they always **did**.

But **thinking** about it, thought Norm, thinking about it, something else **equally** unthinkable had just happened. Or rather, something else equally unthinkable **hadn't** just happened. Because for once, Chelsea – aka The World's Most Annoying Next Door Neighbour – **hadn't** popped up on the other side of the fence the moment Norm had set foot on the drive. Which wasn't just **unusual**. It was completely **unheard** of, as far as Norm could remember. Which admittedly wasn't **all** that long. But that wasn't the point. The point was that Chelsea **always** appeared whenever Norm so much as stuck a **toe** outside his front door. It was as if she was watching his every move on CCTV cameras so that she knew precisely when to pounce. Like some kind of hi-tech spider, waiting for a poor unsuspecting fly to land on her web. But for some reason, on this particular occasion, Chelsea **hadn't** pounced. So

 how come? wondered Norm. Because there must have been a flipping good reason. Not that he was **bothered**, of course. Quite the opposite, in fact. He was completely **unbothered**. But it was still a bit puzzling.

Gordon flipping **Bennet**, thought Norm. Just **thinking** about why Chelsea hadn't suddenly appeared like she **normally** did, was **bothering** him. Even when she wasn't **there**, she was **still** flipping annoying! **That's** how annoying Chelsea was!

Not for the *first* time, Norm had set off without any clear idea of where he was setting off *for*. Or any idea at *all*, for that matter. Like a leaf floating down a river, he was simply going with the flow. And not for the *first* time, he'd been so lost in thought that he hadn't realised where he'd flowed to. By the time

Norm snapped out of it and *did* realise, he realised that he was only just around the corner from his old house. Which therefore meant that he was also only a couple of minutes from *Mikey's* house. Because unlike him, *Mikey* hadn't had to move to a house a million times smaller, with paper-thin walls and only *one* flipping toilet! And even though Mikey had "got stuff on" and couldn't go biking, there was no harm calling in, was there? Just in case? Well, according to *Chelsea*, Mikey had "got stuff on", anyway. Exactly what kind of stuff was anybody's guess. And quite why **Chelsea** would know about it was anybody's guess, as well. Since when had Chelsea and Mikey ever been friends? wondered Norm. Why would **Mikey** be doing stuff that **he** didn't know about – but Chelsea did? It

just didn't make sense. But that didn't matter, thought Norm. Because if you couldn't just drop in on your best friend, who **could** you just drop in on? And if he **was** out? So what? With any luck, Mikey's mum might offer to make him some hot chocolate while he waited. And frankly, that would **more** than make up for Mikey not being in. Because never mind the **food** of gods, Mikey's mum's hot chocolate was the stuff of flipping **legend**. Smooth and delicious and oh, so **sweet**. Topped off with squirty cream and sprinkles. It was heaven in a mug.

Before he knew it, Norm had reached Mikey's house, got off his bike and rung the bell. What would he do if it was actually Mikey who came to the door? He hadn't had time to think about it. What would he say? Would he just come straight out with it and ask Mikey what was going on? Because the more Norm thought about it, the more he didn't like it. What if Mikey and Chelsea were …

Norm managed to stop himself just in time. Because of all the unthinkable things he'd **not** thought about, **that** was by far **the** most unthinkable. Which presumably was why he'd somehow managed to block it out of his mind and **not** think about it. Until now. They couldn't be, could they? Mikey and Chelsea weren't secretly … No, surely not, thought Norm, stopping himself again. That just wasn't possible. They might already be thirteen. But even so. That didn't mean you suddenly had to ...

Norm shuddered violently, like a jelly in a gale force wind. For a split second he honestly thought he was going to puke. But before he **could**, the door opened, revealing **not** Mikey, but Mikey's **dad**.

"NORMAN!!!" bellowed Mikey's dad at the top of his voice, as if Norm was standing on the other side of the Grand Canyon, instead of just in front of him.

Norm pulled a face. "Hi, Mikey's dad."

"HOW ARE YOU, NORMAN?"

"Fine, thanks," said Norm automatically, despite the ringing sensation in his ears.

"EXCELLENT, NORMAN! GOOD TO SEE YOU, NORMAN!"

Gordon flipping **Bennet**, thought Norm. Did Mikey's dad not **realise** how loud he was shouting? It was like being stuck in the front row of a concert by one of those old bands **his** dad liked. And how come he kept saying his name every two seconds? Was it to remind **himself** what Norm's name was? Or was it to remind **Norm** what his name was? Either way, thought Norm, it was getting flipping annoying.

"SO WHAT CAN I DO FOR YOU, NORMAN?"

"Er, I was just wondering if Mikey was in?" said Norm.

"WHAT'S THAT, NORMAN? YOU WERE WONDERING IF MIKEY WAS IN, NORMAN?"

Norm nodded.

"NO, NORMAN! MIKEY'S **NOT** IN, NORMAN!!!"

"Oh hello, Norman," said Mikey's mum, appearing in the doorway.

"Hi, Mikey's mum," said Norm.

"What a **lovely** surprise. I had no idea at all that you were here."

Seriously? thought Norm. Because he was pretty sure that everyone within a five-mile flipping **radius** knew that he was here by now. In fact, never mind a five-mile radius, there were probably goat herders in darkest Peru who knew that he was here by now.

Not that Norm knew whether there actually **were** any goat herders in Peru. **Or** whether it was particularly dark there. But that wasn't the point. The point was, he found it hard to believe that Mikey's mum hadn't heard Mikey's dad yelling and bawling like some kind of demented human foghorn.

"I was just saying to Norman here, that unfortunately Mikey isn't home at the moment," said Mikey's dad, finally – and mercifully, for the sake of Norm's eardrums – lowering his voice to something approaching normal conversational level.

"What?" said Mikey's mum. "Er, no, that's right.

He's not in. Definitely."

Definitely*?** thought Norm. Why did Mikey's mum feel the need to add ***that*?** Mikey was either ***in*,** or he ***wasn't in. So a straight ***no*** would have been sufficient. It was ***almost*** as if Mikey's mum and dad were trying to ***hide*** something from him. But why would they do that? Mikey's mum and dad didn't have a devious bone in their bodies, between

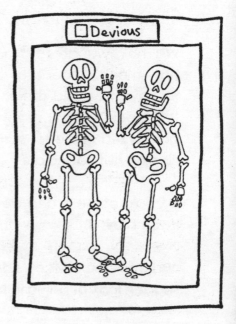

them. Or at least Norm ***presumed*** that they didn't, anyway. Because Mikey ***definitely*** didn't have a devious bone in ***his*** body. So it seemed only logical that his ***parents*** didn't, either.

"We'll tell him you called though," said Mikey's dad. "Won't we, dear?"

"Er, yes," said Mikey's mum. "Of course we will."

"He'll be very disappointed when he finds out he missed you."

Will he? wondered Norm. And just how much longer was he going to have to stand there, like a total doughnut, before he got invited inside for some flipping hot chocolate?

"I could come in and wait, if you like?"

"Pardon?" said Mikey's dad, a sudden look of panic in his eyes.

"I said I could come in and wait?" repeated Norm. "Just till Mikey gets back?"

"Erm, no sorry, Norman," said Mikey's mum. "But that's not possible today."

"No, that's right, Norman," said Mikey's dad. "Stuff to do. You know how it is?"

Norm sniffed a couple of times.

"Something wrong?" said Mikey's mum, anxiously.

"Is that ... **_chocolate_** I can smell?" said Norm, hopefully.

"What?" said Mikey's dad, quickly. "No, no. I don't think so. Do you, dear?"

"What?" said Mikey's mum. "No, definitely not chocolate."

Definitely not chocolate? thought Norm. Again, why **_definitely_**?

"Well, don't let us keep you, Norman," said Mikey's dad. "I'm sure you must have lots of stuff to do, too."

"Not really, no," said Norm. Which was true. He had no stuff to do at all. Well, apart from finding out what the heck Mikey and Chelsea were up to.

"Oh," said Mikey's dad. "Well, I'm sure your parents must be wondering where you are."

"Not really, no," said Norm again. Which was **also** true. Because as far as his **parents** were concerned, he was supposed to be at home, looking after his smelly little brothers, not here, dropping hints to be asked in for hot chocolate. Hints which appeared to be having no effect whatso-flipping-ever. So, thinking about it, thought Norm, thinking about it, perhaps it was time to accept defeat and start heading back again.

Which – after saying goodbye to Mikey's mum and dad and getting back on his bike – was precisely what Norm did.

CHAPTER 12

Going home, at that **particular** moment, wasn't very high on Norm's list of priorities. Not that going home was ever all that high on Norm's list of priorities. And not that Norm actually **had** a list of priorities, anyway. But even if he **did**, going home would definitely be somewhere down towards the bottom. Way below getting his brothers adopted, way, **way** below introducing legislation to make it illegal to be Chelsea and way, way, **way** below becoming World Mountain Biking Champion. Not that **that** seemed very

likely right now, what with a) hardly spending any time actually biking and b) having a rubbish bike to actually bike **on**. Well, maybe not a **completely** rubbish bike. But one which, in Norm's opinion, would undoubtedly benefit from having new front fork suspension fitted. Along with new handlebars. And maybe some new pedals. And a new pair of wheels. Other than **that** though, it was perfectly rideable. Well, apart from the actual frame. Which basically just left the seat. But he couldn't very well just ride around on a flipping **seat**, could he? And frankly, thought Norm, if he **could** just ride around on a seat, he'd be better off joining a flipping **circus**. And anyway, occasionally pedalling over to

Mikey's house, or pootling along to the allotments, hardly counted as **riding**, as far as **Norm** was concerned. Not **proper** riding, anyway. He was a **mountain** biker, not a flipping **molehill** biker. Not that there were any **mountains** anywhere near the town where he lived. Just a small hill behind the shopping precinct. Which was better than nothing. Just. But unless Norm got to practise there regularly, he was never going to get any better. And if he was never ever going to get any better, he was never ever going to achieve his ultimate goal. In which case he might as well give up biking altogether and take up another hobby instead, like beekeeping, or synchronised sewing.

Home sweet flipping home

Despite all that though, it was definitely time for Norm to go home. He might not have **liked** it, but he knew that it was the **right** thing to do. And just occasionally, even **Norm** did the right thing, if somewhat grudgingly. Or in this case, so grudgingly that if he'd been pedalling any slower, he'd have been going backwards.

On the plus side, Chelsea still wasn't home. Or at least, Norm **assumed** that she wasn't. Because amazingly, for the **second** time that day, she **didn't** magically materialise like a genie from a bottle the moment he appeared on the drive. Which, on one hand, was brilliant, obviously. But on the other hand, it did make Norm wonder, once again, what the heck Chelsea could possibly be up to. And more disturbingly, what Chelsea and Mikey could possibly be up to, **together**.

"Well, well, well," said Grandpa when Norm eventually walked into the kitchen. "Look who it is."

Norm pulled a face. Surely it couldn't have been **that** much of a surprise, could it? After all, he did **live** here. It wasn't as if a complete **stranger** had just wandered in, off the street. Imagine how astonished Grandpa would be if **that** ever happened.

"You're welcome, by the way," said Grandpa, before Norm had the chance to reply.

"Uh?" said Norm. "What for?"

"What do you mean, what for?" said Grandpa. "For looking after your brothers, you numpty."

"Oh right, yeah," said Norm. "Thanks, Grandpa. I forgot."

"You forgot that I was looking after your brothers?" said Grandpa, uncertainly.

"No," said Norm. "I just forgot to say thanks, that's all."

"I don't know," said Grandpa with a weary shake of his head. "What are we going to do with you, Norman?"

Norm thought for a moment. What was **who** going to do with him? Who exactly did Grandpa mean, by **we**? And what had it got to do with **them**, anyway?

"They're not here, in case you're wondering," said Grandpa, derailing Norm's train of thought.

"Who aren't?" said Norm.

"Your brothers."

"WHAAAAAT?" honked Norm, like a startled seal. If Brian and Dave weren't here, where on earth **were** they? His parents were going to go abso-flipping-lutely **ballistic** when they found out!

218

And one thing was for sure. **Norm** would get the blame.

"Just joking," said Grandpa.

"Uh?" said Norm. "What do you mean?"

"I mean your mum and dad aren't here yet," said Grandpa, his eyes crinkling in the corners. "Your brothers are upstairs."

Norm puffed out his cheeks, like a hamster stuffing its pouch, before slowly exhaling.
He hadn't felt **this** relieved since the time he'd woken up and realised he'd only **dreamt** he'd been standing at a supermarket checkout, totally naked.

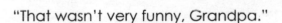

"That wasn't very funny, Grandpa."

"Oh, come on," said Grandpa. "Where's your sense of humour?"

Norm had no *idea* where his sense of humour was. It could be lost down the back of the flipping sofa, for all *he* knew. *Or* cared. What Norm was *much* more concerned by was the fact that, just for a *few* short seconds, he'd

genuinely been worried where his little brothers were. Was this yet *another* sign that he was getting older? And anyway, Norm already *knew* that his parents weren't here yet, because their stupid little car wasn't parked outside their stupid little house when he'd got back just now. So it was a pretty pointless joke in the *first* flipping place.

"You're back, then, Norman?" said Dave, appearing in the doorway.

"Well, obviously," said Brian, appearing next to Dave. "Unless it's a hologram."

Gordon flipping **Bennet**, thought Norm. Was it too late to sneak back out again?

"Sorry by the way, Norman," said Brian.

"What for?" said Norm.

"For eating all the pizza."

"WHAAAAAT?" said Norm.

"I'm not sorry," said Dave. "I'm quite glad actually."

"WOOF!" went John, trotting into the kitchen, tail wagging furiously, as if he was conducting an orchestra.

"You're **right**, John," said Brian. "It **was** yummy, wasn't it?"

Norm stared at Brian for a moment, unsure what he was more amazed by. The fact that Brian was still convinced he could understand what John was *saying* – or what he was convinced that John had just *said*?

"Seriously?" said Norm. "You gave the flipping *dog* some pizza? But you didn't think of saving any for *me*?"

Brian shrugged. "Well, we *thought* about it."

"But you didn't actually *do* it?" said Norm.

"Correct," said Brian.

Norm sighed.

"Actually, it was *Dave's* idea," said Brian.

Norm immediately swivelled around and fixed Dave with the evillest glare that he could muster. But it didn't have the desired effect. Quite the opposite, in fact. Dave just grinned.

"You got a problem with that?"

Had he got a **problem** with that? thought Norm. Yes, he had a flipping problem with that. Who **wouldn't** have a flipping problem with that? But it was pretty obvious, now, that Dave saw this as some kind of payback. For Norm **not** paying for the pizza. But it wasn't **Norm's** fault Grandpa had paid for it instead.

"Are we quits, now?" said Norm.

"Yeah, we're quits," said Dave.

"Quits for **what**?" said Brian.

"That's for you to know and me to find out," said Norm.

Brian pulled a face. "Don't you mean the other way round?"

"Uh?" said Norm.

"Don't you mean that's for **me** to know and **you** to find out?" said Brian.

Gordon flipping **Bennet**, thought Norm. And to think that, just a few seconds ago, he'd actually **cared** where his brothers were. Now it was business as flipping usual. But at least he knew where he stood with Dave. Dave knew that Norm had abandoned them earlier and gone out on his bike, when he shouldn't have. And the price, for Dave **not** telling his mum and dad, was **pizza**. OK, so it was a pretty monu-flipping-**mental** price to pay. But if it meant his mum and dad not finding out, it would be worth every single bite.

A car pulled up outside the house. A horn tooted. A couple of doors slammed. Norm shot Dave an anxious glance. Would he keep his side of the bargain, or not?

"Don't worry, Norman," said Dave, as if he'd been reading Norm's mind. "Your secret's safe with me."

"What secret?" said Brian.

"If I told you, it wouldn't be a secret, would it?" said Dave.

Brian sighed. "That's not *fair*."

"Welcome to my world," said Norm.

CHAPTER 13

"We're home!" yelled Norm's dad, from the hallway.

"No, **really**?" muttered Norm, sarcastically.

"Don't be like **that**, Norman," said Grandpa.

Norm pulled a face. "Like **what**?"

"Like **that**," said Grandpa.

"Well, it's **obvious** they're home," said Norm. "He didn't have to actually **say** it."

"It's not obvious," said Brian. "Might have been burglars."

Gordon flipping **Bennet**, thought Norm. It **might** have been a confused badger. But it **wasn't**, was it? And anyway, if it **was** burglars, they'd have to be pretty flipping **desperate**, breaking into **this** house. Because there was nothing worth  nicking here. They'd be better off burgling a flipping **skip**.

"Are you going to go now, Grandpa?" said Dave.

"Why?" said Grandpa.

"Because Mum and Dad are back?"

"Are you trying to get rid of me?" said Grandpa, his eyes crinkling slightly in the corners.

"No, **course** not, Grandpa!" wailed Dave.

"Hmmm," said Grandpa, thoughtfully. "Well, in that case I think I might hang around a bit longer, if that's OK?"

"YAY!!!" sang Brian and Dave, in unison.

"WOOF!" went John.

"Yes, I **know** that you're happy Grandpa's staying, too," cooed Brian, crouching down and ruffling John's fur. "Yes, you **are**, aren't you? Yes, you **are**! Because you're a **good** boy, aren't you? Yes, you **are**!"

Grandpa gave Norm a quick glance. But it was long enough. It told Norm **all** he needed to know. That Grandpa could feel his pain. That he knew **exactly** what Norm was going through. Because **Grandpa** had gone through it himself, once upon a time. **He'd** had little brothers, too. Although, presumably, **one** of them hadn't been convinced that he could talk to a half-Polish dog named after one of the Beatles. Because, apart from anything, the Beatles hadn't even been **invented** then. But that wasn't the point. The point was that when it came to being driven around the bend, Grandpa had been there, done that and got the flipping T-shirt.

"NORMAN?!" yelled Norm's dad.

"YEAH?" yelled Norm.

"COME HERE!"

"WHY?" yelled Norm.

"NEVER MIND **WHY**! JUST DO IT!"

"BUT ..." began Norm.

"COME HERE!" yelled his dad.

Norm sighed, as if he'd just been told to go and hoover the lawn.

"**NOW**!"

"All right, all right," huffed Norm, trudging reluctantly towards the door.

"Yeah, Norman," grinned Brian.

"Yeah, Norman," grinned Dave.

"Shut up!" hissed Norm.

230

"I hope you weren't talking to **me**," said his dad, when Norm appeared in the hall, a moment later.

"What?" said Norm. "No, no. Course not, Dad. I was talking to Brian and Dave. Honest."

"Good," said Norm's dad.

Norm couldn't help noticing that his dad was holding a couple of supermarket carrier bags in each hand.

"Well?" said Norm's dad impatiently. "Don't just stand there."

Uh? thought Norm. If he couldn't stand **here**, where was he **supposed** to flipping stand? And how come his dad wanted to see him so urgently? Not just to tell him **that**, surely? And surely not to help carry all those bags into the kitchen, either? Not all by himself, anyway. What did his dad think this was? Flipping **medieval** times, or something? Not that they actually **had** supermarkets in medieval times, of

course. Or at least Norm didn't **think** that they did. But that wasn't the point. The point was ...

Norm stopped trying to think what the point was and started gawping, like a penguin outside a fish shop. Not at the actual carrier bags, but what appeared to be **in** them. Every single **one** of them.

"Are they ..."

"Are they what, love?" said Norm's mum, walking through the front door, carrying even **more** bags.

"What I ... **think** they are?" said Norm, as if he hardly dared say what he **thought** they were. Just in case it turned out that the whole thing was some kind of optical illusion.

"That all depends," said Norm's mum.

Norm pulled a face. "On what?"

"On what you **think** they are?"

"Coco Pops?" said Norm, tentatively.

Norm's mum nodded.

"But ..." began Norm.

"What?" said Norm's dad. "We told you we'd get some, didn't we?"

Yeah, *some*, thought Norm. But this was enough to feed a small *army*. Not that he knew exactly how many boxes of Coco Pops it took to feed an army. Or even roughly. And not that he was complaining, either.

"You were the one who made all the fuss, Norman."

"Yeah, I know, Dad, but ..."

Norm suddenly froze, mid-sentence, as if someone had pulled a plug out.

"What's the matter, love?" said his mum. "You look like you've just seen a ghost."

But what Norm had just seen was *much* more shocking than a ghost.

234

"Are they ..."

"Are they **what**, love?"

"**Actual** Coco Pops?"

Norm's mum nodded again.

"Not supermarket own-brand ones?"

"Nope," said Norm's mum.

"Real, **actual** Coco Pops?" said Norm, as if he **still** couldn't quite believe his own eyes.

Norm's mum laughed. "Real, **actual**, one hundred per cent **genuine** Coco Pops."

"Flipping heck," blurted Norm, before he could stop himself.

"Language!" said his dad.

But Norm's dad didn't seem terribly cross. On the contrary, he looked suspiciously like he, too, was trying not to laugh.

"They were on special offer," explained Norm's mum.

"Yeah, but even so," said Norm.

"What, love?"

"Well ... they still must have cost quite a lot of money."

"What are you saying, son?" said Norm's dad.

Norm shrugged. "I thought we were supposed to be skint."

"Ah, yes," said his dad. "About that."

About *what*? thought Norm. What was *that* supposed to mean? Surely, they either were *skint*, or they *weren't* skint. Unless his parents had been secretly living a life of *luxury* all this time and had only been *pretending* that all they could afford

was cheap, supermarket own-brand Coco Pops, instead of **proper** ones. But what kind of sick, twisted mind would even **think** about doing something like **that**? Because that wouldn't merely be **unfair**, it would be **inhumane**.

"We might not be for too much longer."

"Might not be **what**?" said Norm.

"Skint," said his dad.

Uh? thought Norm. His dad **did** actually know what "skint" meant, didn't he? Or was he getting it mixed up with something else entirely?

"I've got a job."

Norm couldn't have been more shocked if his dad had suddenly sprouted an extra head and started tap dancing.

"What your father **meant** was that he **might** have got a job," said Norm's mum.

"I've had two interviews," said his dad.

"Even so, love. We don't want to build our hopes up too much."

But it was **way** too late for **that**. **Norm's** hopes were already sky high. Frankly, if they got any **higher**, he was going to get vertigo.

Norm's mum smiled. "Let's just say ... things can only get better."

HOPE

Not necessarily, thought Norm. Because in **his** experience, things **could** actually get worse. And they usually flipping **did**. And even if they did get **better**, they only got better for a little while, before immediately getting worse again. Usually **much** worse. So until he knew for **sure** whether his dad had got a job or not, he was going to have to at least **try** and keep his feet on the ground. Because if his dad **had** got a job? Well, that could change **everything**. Well, maybe not everything. That depended on what job it was, of course. Not that Norm had ever really known what his dad had done anyway. He might have been a flipping **spaceman**, for all **he** knew. Or cared. As long as he was being paid for doing whatever it was that he was doing, **that** was all that mattered.

"Is that where you've been, then?" said Norm. "For an interview?"

Norm's mum and dad exchanged a quick glance.

"Er, no," said Norm's mum. "Not *exactly*."

Norm pulled a face. "Not exactly?"

Norm's dad nodded. "Not exactly."

"So where *have* you been, then?" said Norm.

"Where *have* we been?" said Norm's dad.

"Yeah," said Norm.

"Why do you want to know?"

Norm shrugged. "No reason."

"No reason?"

"I just want to know, that's all, Dad."

"That's all?"

Norm sighed. Was his dad going to repeat *everything* he said? Because if so, this could take some time.

"We've been to the supermarket, love," said Norm's mum. "Obviously."

"Yeah, I know," said Norm. "But apart from that."

"Apart from that?" said his dad.

Gordon flipping Bennet, thought Norm. It was like being stuck in a lift, with a flipping **parrot**! Not that he'd ever actually **been** stuck in a lift with a parrot before. But that wasn't the point.

The point was, if someone didn't hurry up and tell him where they'd been – **exactly**, or even **roughly** – the flipping Coco Pops would be past their flipping best-before date before he got the chance to flipping **eat** them!

Norm's mum and dad looked at each other for a moment.

"Shall I tell him?" said Norm's mum.

"Do you **want** to?" said Norm's dad.

"I don't mind," said his mum.

"Well, I don't mind, either," said his dad, with a shrug.

Someone please tell me, thought Norm. And preferably **today**.

"You **really** want to know where we've been, Norman?" said Norm's dad.

Norm nodded.

"Apart from the supermarket?"

Norm nodded again.

"It's funny you should ask, actually, love," said his mum.

"Is it?" asked Norm, who couldn't imagine why it might be even **remotely** funny. "Why's that, then?"

"Because we can't say."

Seriously? thought Norm. After all **that?** They couldn't say? Or **wouldn't** say? Or maybe **could** say, but **shouldn't** say? Either flipping way, it was unbe-flipping-**lievable**.

"Well?" said Norm's dad.

"What?" said Norm.

"Are you going to give us a hand with these bags, or what?"

"Do I have a choice?" said Norm.

"Not really, no," said his dad.

Gordon flipping **Bennet**, thought Norm. So why flipping **ask**, then?

CHAPTER 14

Norm was just about to take a mouthful of Coco Pops when the doorbell rang. Which under **normal** circumstances wouldn't have been so bad. But these were **far** from normal circumstances. Because not only was he about to take a mouthful of real, **actual**, one hundred per cent **genuine** Coco Pops, instead of the usual cheapo supermarket own-brand ones, he was still only halfway through his third bowl. And after waiting all **this** time, Norm had every intention of having at least two more. Bowlfuls. Not mouthfuls.

The doorbell rang again.

"WELL?" yelled Norm's dad, from the front room. "IS SOMEONE GOING TO GET THAT, OR NOT?"

Norm knew **one** thing for sure. There was no flipping way **he** was going to get it. Not now. Or **ever**, if he could possibly help it. Why **should** he? Why couldn't one of his stupid little brothers do it? Or Grandpa? It wasn't like **he** had anything better to do. Or his mum, for that matter. It wasn't like **she** had anything better to do, either. She was probably just sat in front of the TV, endlessly zapping between shopping channels, same as flipping usual.

Come to think of it, thought Norm, why couldn't his **dad** get the flipping door, instead of bawling like a baboon with bellyache? Would that **really** be too much trouble?

Hmmm?

"NORMAN?" yelled Norm's dad, even louder.

"YEAH?" Norm yelled back.

"ANSWER THE DOOR!"

"BUT ..."

"NO BUTS!" yelled his dad. "I SAID, ANSWER THE DOOR! NOW!!!"

Gordon flipping **Bennet**, thought Norm, getting up from the table. He might have flipping known **he'd** end up having to do it. He could have been on the other side of the flipping **world** and he'd have **still** ended up having to flipping do it.

"AND NORMAN?"

"YEAH?" yelled Norm, heading for the hall, more slowly than an arthritic snail.

"THERE'S NO NEED TO SHOUT!"

Norm sighed, seemingly resigned to his fate. The only surprise, as far as *he* was concerned, was that just for the very briefest of moments he'd actually believed there might have been a **different** outcome – and that someone **else** might have gone to see who was at the door. Maybe in a parallel universe somewhere, they **would** have. In fact, thought Norm, maybe in a parallel universe somewhere there was another **version** of him, living a completely **opposite** life. A life where **nothing** was ever unfair. A life that always made perfect sense. A life of doing whatever you wanted to do, **whenever** you wanted to **do** it. Meanwhile back on earth, in the world of Norm – or in the world of *this* Norm, anyway – **nothing** was fair and **nothing** made any sense whatso-flipping-**ever**. As for *this* Norm, being allowed to do whatever he wanted, whenever he wanted to do it? There was more chance of him becoming Prime Minister than there was of *that* ever happening.

The doorbell rang once again. Whoever it was would have known there was someone in because of all the yelling.

"All right, all right," muttered Norm to himself. "Keep your flipping hair on."

There was only a split second of silence once Norm had opened the door. But it was long enough to reveal not only a beaming **Mikey** standing on the other side of it, but an equally beaming **Chelsea**, too. And as if that wasn't **sufficiently** unexpected already, they appeared to be holding a cake between them. A cake with far too many candles on it and the words, "Happy Flipping Birthday" scrawled in icing.

"SURPRISE!!!" shrieked Mikey and Chelsea, in unison.

Norm pulled a face. "But ..."

"What's the matter, **Norman**?" said Chelsea.

"My birthday's **next** Saturday."

"Yeah, we know," said Chelsea.

"What?" said Norm.

"*That's* the surprise!" said Mikey.

"Uh?" said Norm. "Oh, right."

"Hope you like it, Norm. It's a chocolate cake. We made it ourselves!"

"Wait," said Norm. "So ... is that what you've been doing, today?"

"Well, of *course* it is!" grinned Chelsea. "What did you *think* we've been doing, *Norman*?"

"Er, nothing," said Norm quickly. But at least that explained why Mikey's house had smelled so deliciously chocolatey earlier on. *And* why Mikey's parents had been acting so flipping *weirdly*. Mikey and Chelsea had been *inside*, making a *cake*! And it was all a big secret! Norm *knew* something had been going on. Thank flipping *goodness* that's all it was!

"Oh, hi, guys," said Norm's mum, appearing in the hall.

"Hi!" chirped Chelsea.

"We made Norm a birthday cake," said Mikey.

"Really?" said Norm's mum. "Well, that was ..."

"A surprise?" said Norm.

"Well, I was *going* to say that it was very thoughtful," said Norm's mum. "But yes. It must have been a surprise. And it looks delicious, too!"

"Thanks," said Mikey.

"What's all this racket?" said Norm's dad, emerging from the front room.

"Look," said Norm's mum. "Mikey and Chelsea made Norman a cake for his birthday. Isn't that thoughtful of them?"

Norm's dad pulled a face. "But his birthday's not till **next** Saturday."

"Yeah, they know that," said Norm. "It was a surprise."

"I'm not **surprised** it was a surprise," said Norm's dad. "Great cake, by the way."

"Thanks," said Mikey.

"Looks good enough to eat."

Uh? thought Norm. What **else** would you do with a flipping cake? Wash your **car** with it?

"YEAH! CAKE!" screamed Brian and Dave, charging headlong down the stairs, like a pair of hyperactive hyenas.

"Yeah," said Norm. "*My* cake, to be precise."

"What?" said Brian.

"Well, *you* two aren't getting any."

"Aw, that is *SO* unfair!" squawked Dave."

"Seriously?" said Norm. "You think *that's* unfair?"

"Don't worry, boys," said Norm's mum. "You'll get some cake."

"Someone mention cake?" said Grandpa, poking his head round the kitchen door. "I'll get the kettle on."

253

Gordon flipping **Bennet**, thought Norm. He'd be lucky to get **any** flipping cake at **this** flipping rate.

"So, what are you going to be doing on your **actual** birthday, Norman?" said Chelsea.

"Dunno," shrugged Norm, not even noticing that, for once, Chelsea hadn't overemphasised his name like she usually did.

"Actually, we were thinking of asking Norman's cousins over," said Norm's dad.

WHAAAAAT? thought Norm. No flipping **way**. Not his perfect flipping **cousins**. Surely **not**. Not on his **birthday**. That would be like all his worst nightmares rolled into one! He'd rather have all his teeth pulled out. **Without** anaesthetic. What were his mum and dad trying to **do**? Scar him for life?

Norm's mum smiled. "He's only teasing, love."

"Really?" said Norm.

"Really," said his mum.

"Promise?" said Norm.

"Promise," said his mum.

Norm felt a sudden and almost overwhelming surge of relief flood through his body. He still had no idea what he was going to be doing on his actual birthday. But it didn't matter now. Because **anything** would be better than **that**. Well, **nearly** anything, anyway.

His mum and dad looked at each other for a moment.

"Do you think we should say?" said Norm's mum.

"I don't know," said his dad. "Do you think we should?"

Not *this* again, thought Norm.

"Remember you asked us where we went, love?" said his mum, eventually.

"Yeah," said Norm.

"Apart from the supermarket?"

Norm nodded.

"Well, we were looking at bikes."

Norm stared vacantly at his mum for several seconds. He'd *heard* what she'd just said, but it was taking a while for him to actually *digest* what she'd just said. Looking at *bikes*? Why on *earth* would his *parents* have been looking at *bikes*? That seemed about as likely as him *volunteering* to go to IKEA. As opposed to being physically *dragged* there, kicking and screaming.

"Did you *hear* your mother, Norman?" said Norm's dad. "She said we were looking at *bikes*."

Norm nodded again.

"At an actual *bike* shop."

"Not for *us*," said Norm's mum.

Norm looked at his mum. "Sorry, what?"

"We weren't looking at bikes for *ourselves*," said Norm's dad.

Norm was beginning to get confused. Or rather, he was beginning to get even *more* confused than he was in the *first* place. And *that* was flipping saying something.

"*Or* your brothers."

"Uh?" said Norm. "You mean ..."

"Yes, love," said Norm's mum, interjecting. "We were looking at bikes for *you*."

It took a few more seconds for the penny to finally drop. But when it *did*, it dropped with such an almighty *clang*, it was a wonder that it didn't set off any nearby car alarms. Not

that Norm would have heard them anyway, what with all the bells and whistles currently going off in his head.

"So, **that's** what we thought we could do, on your actual birthday," said Norm's dad. "Go to a bike shop."

"Your dad and I thought it would be a bit risky to just go ahead and buy you one," said his mum. "So, we thought it would be best if **you** were there, too. After all, **you're** the bike expert. Not **us**."

"Well?" said Norm's dad, after a while. "Aren't you going to **say** something?"

Norm **tried** to say something, but when he opened his mouth what came out, sounded more like a llama with laryngitis than actual words. Then again, it wasn't easy to talk when it felt as if every last drop of air had been sucked out of his lungs by a vacuum cleaner.

"You **would** like a new bike, wouldn't you, love?" said Norm's mum, uncertainly.

"We can always get you something else instead, if you prefer," said his dad.

Seriously? thought Norm. Would he like a new *bike*? He might be getting older. He might be changing ever so slightly. He *might* even be turning into his dad, just a *teensy* bit. But *some* things would never *ever* change.

"Well?" said Norm's mum. "**Would** you?"

Norm grinned. "Abso-flipping-*lutely*!"

More WORLD OF NORM fun!
Try this abso-flipping-lutely great quiz from Norm's activity book ... OUT NOW!

Norm's Family Fun Quiz

Which person or pet in Norm's family is most like you?
Tick the boxes.

The first thing you notice when you wake up in the morning is that...

a. You're totally naked in the middle of a supermarket. Phew – it's only a dream. ☐

b. Your bed's wet – again. ☐

c. You're still alive! ☐

d. The house is really messy and everyone needs to tidy their rooms. ☐

e. You've done a messy poo next to someone's bed. ☐

Whoopee! You are given an iPad for a birthday present. What's the first thing you do with it?

a. Get straight onto YouTube to watch a selection of mountain biking videos. ☐

b. Get straight onto the Lord of the Rings fan site. ☐

c. Fiddle with the iPad for hours trying to work out how it turns on. Then give up and go off to do some gardening. ☐

d. Spend the day doing online shopping. ☐

e. Chew it into tiny little pieces. ☐

Your idea of a really fun afternoon is...

a. Pimping up your bike and building a ramp to ride on. ☐

b. Taking the dog for a walk in the park. ☐

c. Going down the allotment to put some manure on your courgettes. ☐

d. Taking a trip to IKEA and forcing your family to go with you. ☐

e. Running around in circles, while doing SBDs (Silent But Deadlies). ☐

Your favourite food is...

a. Any Wikipizza pizza ☐

b. Mum's cauliflower cheese ☐

c. Anything that doesn't give you wind or get under your false teeth. ☐

d. Anything that you don't have to cook. ☐

e. Anything you can chew on while rooting around the bins. ☐

What's your ambition in life?

a. To become World Mountain Biking Champion. ☐

b. To eat up all your greens and be allowed a pudding afterwards. ☐

c. To grow a massive prize-winning marrow. ☐

d. To win a £10,000 shopping spree in your local department store. ☐

e. To drink from the toilet whenever you feel like it.. ☐

What really upsets you?

a. The unfairness of life. ☐

b. Bullying. ☐

c. Frost ruining your tomatoes. ☐

d. Your online shopping deliveries not arriving on time ☐

e. Being put on a lead. ☐

What sound do you make when you're approaching someone from behind?

a. The whizzing sound of mountain bike wheels, followed by the screech of brakes. ☐

b. The creak of the creaky floorboard behind the computer, as you creep up on whoever's online. ☐

c. A slight panting and shuffling – you're not as young as you used to be. ☐

d. The rustling sound of your carrier bags, groaning with shopping. ☐

e. A loud panting and slurping noise, topped off by a full-blown smelly fart... ☐

CREAK!

What would make your life much better?

a. Tons of gadgets, including a top-of-the-range smartphone and an iPad in the colour of your choice. ☐

b. If your older sibling was nicer to you, and let you go on the computer more often. ☐

c. If you had a brand-new painted wooden shed with a cosy armchair inside it. ☐

d. If you could lie on the sofa all day, drinking coffee and watching TV shopping channels. ☐

e. If the whole world was a giant park in which you could poo as much as you wanted. ☐

What is one of the worst things you've ever done?

a. Secretly kept money that wasn't yours. ☐

b. Took out the batteries from your brother's alarm clock so that he was late for school. ☐

c. You think you did something really naughty when you were at school but it was so long ago, you can't remember anything about it. ☐

d. Spent vast amounts of money on things that you will never use, like extra-small spoons. ☐

e. Eaten an out-of-date pizza and thrown up on the bathroom floor. ☐

It's most embarrassing when...

a. You accidentally call your teacher 'Mum' in front of the whole class. ☐

b. Your dog runs away from you and you have to chase him round the park, shouting. ☐

c. Your shed looks shabby compared to all the others on the allotment. ☐

d. Your massive credit card bills arrive every month. ☐

e. You never get embarrassed, not even when you let off random farts in public places. ☐

RESULTS

Count your answers to see if you got mostly As, Bs, Cs, Ds or Es. Then see who you're most like!

Mostly As
You are most like Norm

You really don't ask for much in life. A decent mountain bike, regular pocket money, a few state-of-the-art gadgets and the occasional pizza are all you really need. But somehow, things never seem to work out for you. Life is just so unfair...

Mostly Bs
You are most like Brian

You're a simple soul who loves being with animals and playing fantasy games, whenever you get the chance to go on the computer. You have a naughty streak though and often get away with your pranks. But if something upsets you, admit it – you can be a bit of a crybaby.

Mostly Cs
You are most like Grandpa

You're never happier than when you're hanging out at the allotment, tending your vegetables. You are wise, patient and helpful, always ready to welcome anyone into your shed who needs advice. There isn't much you don't know about – you've seen it all!

Mostly Ds
You are most like Norm's mum

There's nothing you enjoy more than lounging around on the sofa, browsing through the TV shopping channels and drinking endless cups of coffee. 'Shop till you Drop' is your motto. But sometimes you wonder why you've got so many boxes of stuff you don't need, cluttering up your hall...

Mostly Es
You are most like John the dog

Energetic and fun-loving, you scamper through life without a care in the world, letting off stinky farts whenever you fancy. Personal hygiene may not be your best point but you are extremely loving and affectionate – even if your breath does stink of rancid toilet water...

Gordon flipping Bennet! Can this really be the last ever book from the WORLD OF NORM?!? Never fear, there's a brand new series coming VERY NEARLY SOON from Jonathan Meres ...

WATCH THIS SPACE!

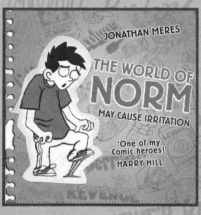

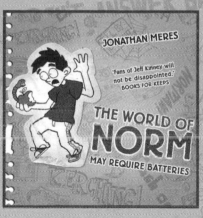

ABOUT THE AUTHOR

Jonathan Meres left school at the age of 16 to join the merchant navy and spent the next seven years sailing around the world having adventures.

Since then he has worked as an ice cream van driver, got a band together, appeared in a pop video and been a stand-up comedian. He's won a *Time Out Award for Comedy* and been nominated for *The Perrier Award* at the Edinburgh Festival.

His hobbies include moaning, doing things, playing things, watching things and embroidery.

Oh, and he's written a little series called **THE WORLD OF NORM ...**